CW00347254

John Llewellyn Probert

JOHN LLEWELLYN PROBERT

John Llewellyn Probert

First published in 2016 by
Horrific Tales Publishing
http://www.horrifictales.co.uk
Copyright © 2015 John Llewellyn Probert

A CIP catalogue record for this book is available
from the British Library

ISBN: 978-1-910283-12-7

CHAPTER ONE

Darkness changes everything.

Sometimes this is a kindness. Light, with all its unyielding brilliance, can be a harsh judge, laying bare the imperfections of the world. Its absence, even if only to a very minor degree, can often leave one with a softer, more pleasant impression of a person, or a place. Imperfections are obscured, irregularities vanish, and the flawed becomes perfection merely with a little assistance from the imagination.

And then there are the bad places. The evil places.

Like a whipped puppy fearful of yet another beating, light shied away from Northcote Park housing estate. During the daytime, the sun remained hidden behind a thick layer of grey cloud that some claimed was pollution from the nearby factories, and others said was smog from the city. But the factories had closed down over ten years ago, and the Clean Air Act had successfully rid the surrounding areas of the suspension of grit and dust that had regularly coated houses, trees, and the linings of lungs, so why not here?

Because it was a place where darkness had taken up residence, some said. And now, having successfully evicted all but the destitute and the desperate, darkness refused to leave.

On this particular June evening the sun was setting over the city, its dying rays turning office blocks and retail parks into geometrical arrangements that radiated a warm and angular beauty. Over Northcote Park, however, the bruised hue of the heavens resembled the colour of mottled skin stretched tight over veins rendered fibrous and unyielding by the application of too many blunt and dirty needles.

3

In the estate's sole recreation area a nervous wind tugged at rusting swings and broken roundabouts. With dogged, foolish persistence it worried at ugly, etiolated weeds that had cracked the rotting concrete of the local playground. The creeping red fungus on their withered leaves mimicked the blood spilled upon this place from the fractured skull of more than one neglected child in times past.

The only lights that burned were petrol fires. The only vehicles in the deserted streets were propped up on bricks. The only voices were the howls of feral animals, emulating their human predecessors with uncanny exactitude as they struggled for existence in tower blocks only all-too-recently vacated.

The old man had chosen the place carefully. Not just because Northcote Park had been a place of misery, violence and deprivation for nearly forty years, but because of what the place had been before that.

Long before that.

His name was Arthur Lipscomb, and he looked like a tramp which, in many ways, is what he was. Both his long grizzled hair and his voluminous, unkempt beard were grey beneath the nicotine stains. Scores of years and thousands of nervously-smoked cigarettes had made both resemble the dirty-yellow stuffing that had burst from the discarded sofa he was at that moment trying to squeeze his frail body past. He had already made it across the playground, tightening the fraying orange binder twine that passed for a belt and prevented his stained raincoat from flapping in the wind. Now he had found his way into Appleton Court blocked by this piece of furniture. Someone had turned the sofa on its end and jammed it diagonally across the doorway so that only rats could get in or out.

He knew it was a warning. He knew that this barrier was not just physical but symbolic, a final attempt to prevent him from going any further. But he had made his mind up long ago, had spent too many years studying, and

4

sacrificed too much of his soul acquiring the necessary items that now lay secure in the dirty canvas bag beneath his right arm, to turn back now.

He pushed at the sagging sofa, only to be rewarded with a worrying creak somewhere at the base of his spine. He had lost so much weight in the last couple of months that what little strength he possessed now threatened to desert him.

But then that's cancer for you, he thought, as he once again applied a scrawny arm to the the torn plastic upholstery. He gave a heave, and the bones of his wrist creaked. A sharp wave of pain warned that if he persisted, the rotting joint would collapse altogether. He looked down. There might just be enough space at the bottom right hand corner for him to crawl through.

Arthur Lipscomb got to his knees. Both swollen joints protested terribly as they hit the ground, the twin demons of arthritis and bone metastases causing him more pain than he should rightly have been able to bear. He ignored the searing, throbbing agony as best he could. He had denied himself the morphine his doctors had told him to take because it was important for his faculties to remain undulled this night, even if it meant the pain would soon become even worse. Instead, all he did was emit a groan as he took the bag from his shoulder and flattened himself on the dirt-streaked concrete, brushing away rat droppings and other animal waste, all of it so close to his face he could smell the rank odour of their leavings.

He took out a battered torch and switched it on. A thready, intermittent beam of light from the cheap and failing battery permitted him glimpses of the rubbish-strewn interior, as well as the scurrying shadows of some of the building's new permanent residents as they fled from the intruder in their midst.

The old man pushed the bag ahead of him, forcing it through the gap between the sofa and the floor. As the bag reached the limit of his outstretched arm it hit something,

5

disturbing a crowd of tiny insects that buzzed angrily and swarmed at his face, speckling his already ravaged features with tiny bites, flying up his nose and into his open mouth. He had to both spit and sneeze to get them out, encasing the pests in tiny prisons of infected mucus that joined the other excrescences on the ground. Once he was sure they were gone, he took a deep breath.

Time to go through.

He tried to stretch his arms ahead of him, but the gnawing pain in his left shoulder was too much to bear. He couldn't allow it to stop him, though, and so he reached over with his right hand and, gripping his left elbow tightly, pulled it towards his body.

The crack of his shoulder fracturing echoed off the surrounding buildings, and the ensuing grinding of the broken bone fragments against one another caused him to scream out loud.

When the pain had died back to an almost tolerable level, Arthur gingerly flexed his fingers. He could still move them, even though his shoulder joint was probably ruined. He gently lifted his left arm up above his head, and gave another scream of pain that was sucked up by the porous concrete.

Wriggling, sliding, groping, struggling, the old man slowly made it through the tiny gap, pushing at the floor with feet clad in boots that were three sizes too large to accommodate the tender fungoid growth on his left ankle, the one he had bandaged up as best he could before coming here. Eventually he was through and shining the torch about him to look for the way upstairs.

It was relatively easy going for the first three flights, but from then on he had to pick his way over crumbling plaster and exposed steel. The beam flickered in the darkness revealing flashes of the graffiti that covered the walls. Every now and then, in amongst the obscenities, accusations and declarations of gang war, he spotted one of the sigils that reassured him he was on the right path.

It was nearly two years since he had seen the first one. They were never obvious, and he had quickly understood that they were not intended for everyone. The sigils could take many forms. Sometimes they would be hidden within the bright colours of a billboard hoarding, others might be woven into the rhythms of music heard emanating from a nightclub at 3am (that time was always significant) and, of course, there were the special messages, the ones that he believed had been left just for him. Scratches on brickwork, cracks on paving stones, and the fingermarks. Especially the fingermarks. He had seen them arranged in complex, smeared patterns on doors, on windows, and on the body of that girl he had discovered one night near the river. He had fled in panic before realising he had been meant to take greater note of the bruising on her neck and body, of the blood streaks that had been arranged to embellish the message that was being conveyed to him. Since then he had been on the lookout for anything that could be a communication, the slightest suggestion that he was on the right path. And eventually the sigils he had found and the rituals he had been required to perform had led him here, to the place where all his efforts would come to fruition.

He hoped.

The way onto the fifth floor landing was clogged with filth. Arthur kicked at it, unleashing a barrage of angry scuttling noises so loud that, for a moment, he teetered backward in shock. The torch helped to scatter a few more of the things that had been hiding in the blackness, and when the sounds died down he gingerly stepped over the still-crawling pile.

Finally, he was there.

The pain in his shoulder had subsided to a dull throb. He knew the slightest movement would bring back the agony, so he swung the bag onto his good shoulder before using the torch to give him a better view of what lay before him.

The fifth floor of Appleton Court, the residential block that lay at the very centre of Northcote Park housing estate, had always been a place of horror. From the moment the building had opened in the early 1970s, people had succumbed to horrible fates there. Babies had suffocated in their cots, men had been electrocuted by faulty electrical equipment, and the suicide rate amongst young women had been abnormally high. But the highest death rate had been amongst the under fives. A slew of infant deaths from every kind of household accident imaginable had prompted many to claim Northcote Park's appalling child safety record to be the inspiration behind the BBC's decision to broadcast its now infamous series of public information films during that decade. Families throughout the country had suddenly found themselves being warned of the dangers of pans of boiling chip fat, the hanging flex from an electric iron, or the precariously balanced heavy object on a kitchen counter, all of which a curious four year old was capable of pulling on top of themselves and causing horrific injuries.

Families everywhere saw the films, but it was the residents of Appleton Court who knew a child who had died in each and every situation depicted in them, and several that had been denied broadcast owing to their nature being even more upsetting.

By the end of the decade the fifth floor lay empty. The families who lived there had preferred to take their chances on the streets rather than risk whatever lay in wait for their children. In 1980, a new scheme created by the then newly-appointed conservative-run city council attempted to force residents into the vacant apartments by significantly reducing their unemployment benefits if they refused to comply. Even with the threat of homelessness hanging over their heads, not a single family could be convinced to move in.

Allowed neither a cure nor a swift amputation, whatever pestilence had infected the fifth floor began to go further. Some claimed it had already been affecting others long before people had begun to vacate the floors above and below the fifth for fear of their lives, and especially the lives of their children.

By the late 1990s the housing project that was Appleton Court was empty, home only to the addicted and the utterly desperate, many of whom went in and never came out again. Not that there was anybody to miss them. There it stood, surveying the city around it with a hundred sightless eyes, a hollow monolith of rotting concrete, rusting iron and crumbling plaster standing on top of the hill on which the estate had been built.

Two thousand years ago, another monolith had stood in its place. That one had been made of blue stone, but had been no less blood-smeared, no less soaked in pain and misery, and no less feared by those who made obeisance to it.

Two thousand years, and yet so little had changed. Or at least Arthur Lipscomb hoped.

In fact he was counting on it.

The cheap plasterboard partitions that had been considered a reasonable substitute for walls had long since rotted, moistened by the damp, and collapsed to form breeding grounds for tiny wriggling creatures that loved the wet. Unsupported, the thin plywood doors had fallen in too, although splintered remnants still remained to mark their passing. The old man avoided all the jagged fragments he could, and tried not to cry out when his foot slid on slime, or when something sharp nearly pierced his ragged soles.

As he made his way across the wasteland of the fifth floor, the old man's torch picked out the remains of the human life that had deserted it so long ago. Rusting valves had caused taps to leak the hard water common to the area until the supply was finally turned off, with the subsequent buildup of calcium carbonate turning sinks and baths into weird, unearthly shapes that now beckoned to him with stalagmitic claws. The low ceiling was a mess of holes. Some were needle-fine, others looked as if they had been punched out by angry fists bigger than any man's. In the corners hung cobwebs, their silken strands dull to the reflected light. Every now and then he glimpsed a fat, hairy body surrounded by the tiny shrivelled corpses of its larder. If nothing else could thrive here, at least the spiders were growing fat. Too fat. The old man kept away from them as best he could, knowing that the plop of one landing on his head and crawling down his neck before he had time to brush it off would be sufficient for him to lose his nerve.

Arthur looked around him. He needed empty floor space in which to work, and he was going to have to clear it himself. A full moon had risen and now, as he had calculated, its light had reached the building. He switched off the torch and waited for his eyes to adjust. Tattered wisps of curtains still remained at a few of the windows, causing creeping, twitching shadows to be cast on the floor as the breeze plucked and toyed with them. He was about to go over and tear them down before he remembered the things he had seen moving over the stained and broken wainscotting and thought better of it.

He waited for the moon to rise a little higher and flood the rubbish-strewn space with a silvery glow. A few of the creatures fled from it, while others - spiders, cockroaches, and other things with segmented bodies and tiny legs that Arthur thought looked wrong - seemed to welcome its arrival, moving out of their webs, scuttling from their burrows and nests to greet this unearthly source of light. He saw antennae raised as if in welcome before he realised they were predators most likely probing the air for the tiny flying creatures the moonlight attracted.

Trying to ignore the things that crawled across the ground, the old man picked up a piece of rotten plywood, shook off whatever clung to it, and began to use it as a shovel, pushing away the rubbish and clearing a space that was roughly circular and with a diameter equal to his own height. He ignored the protesting hissings and scuttlings, steeling himself to crush any living thing that dared remain within.

Now for the next step.

He swung the bag from his shoulder, and rummaged amongst its contents, finally finding what he had been looking for. He didn't want to use the knife, but the blood needed to be fresh. It also had to be his if he was to remain protected from what he was about to call forth.

The blade was as clean as a meat knife taken from a butcher's when the proprietor wasn't looking could be. He had intended to buy one, preferring to cut his flesh with virgin steel, but the money hoarded for the purpose had been stolen yesterday. He knew there would be a risk of infection, but he had rinsed the knife as best he could in hot tap water at the hostel before setting out. Now, in the gleam of the pale light coming through the windows, it looked as pure and unsullied as a knife that had never been used.

As gently as he could, the old man rolled up his left sleeve to just below the elbow. Even the slightest movement of his arm set off cascades of pain that spread down from his broken shoulder and made the fingers of his left hand tingle. He bit his tongue to suppress the urge to scream and, far more importantly, to vomit. He could not afford to lose the valuable ingredients he had consumed to ensure the ritual's success, and any bile he felt rising was ruthlessly swallowed back down and kept there.

He rested the edge of the blade against his wrist and paused for a moment. Before he spilled what little life's blood his tired and failing veins had to offer, it was important that he go over everything he had done to ensure that nothing had been missed, nothing had been forgotten. Delaying things would mean having to wait another month, but that would be better than abject failure tonight and the painful death that would undoubtedly follow.

*

It was the book that had started it all. The crumbling book with a cover like wrinkled skin and a tattered binding that hung in threads from its spine like bare nerve endings primed to cause pain.

It had been small enough to fit in his pocket.

If it hadn't been he would never have taken it. He still firmly believed that. If it had been bigger, or heavier, it would never have slipped from his fingers into the pocket of his raincoat, almost as if it was as eager to escape the place in which he had found it as he had been.

The dying priest's house.

Arthur hadn't known he would find someone close to death when he entered the place, of course. He was just tired and cold as usual, but for a change the alcove in which he had decided to spend the night just happened to have a door that swung open when he leaned against it.

He had still been reticent about entering, but the warm air from the brightly-lit staircase had been so tempting that he had been unable to resist. Just one step inside, he had told himself, just a little way so he could rid his marrow of the chill and then he would go back outside again, shutting the door tightly behind him.

It hadn't quite worked out that way.

One step had become another, and then another. Before he knew it he was climbing the narrow stairs, his broken shoes making little noise on the fraying red carpet that had been inexpertly nailed to the wooden steps beneath.

The door at the top was ajar, and through the crack he had seen a wheezing form on the couch.

That was the only reason he had gone in, he still told himself. The priest (he had seen the black garb and white collar from where he had been crouching) looked as if he might be dying, and to refuse to help someone in distress, especially a man of the cloth, would have been unforgivable.

Arthur had squeezed through the doorway. Opening it any further would have felt like too much of an intrusion. Not that the priest would have noticed. Once Arthur was inside it had quickly become apparent that this particular individual would soon be discovering if his lifelong devotion to the church was going to pay off. The priest's breathing was shallow and every time he inhaled, something deep within his chest made a horrible, croaking rattle. His wrinkled skin was maggot-pale, his eyelids half open to reveal the jaundiced sclerae of dry-looking eyes.

The priest was clutching something.

A book.

An old book.

Possibly a valuable book.

There was nothing that could be done for the dying man - that much was obvious. And if he was on his way out, then he wouldn't be needing any of his worldly possessions. Not where he hoped he was going.

Arthur had looked around the bare room. Aside from the threadbare couch on which the priest was lying, and the two-bar electric fire that filled the place with a cloying warmth that stank of burning dust, there was very little else.

Apart from the book, of course.

It was probably a bible, Arthur thought, a bible or a prayer book. And who was he to deprive a dying priest of something he obviously considered to be so important?

Suddenly, it was no longer important. The priest gave one last, long, drawn out exhalation, coughed a spatter of pink blood onto the pale grey blanket that shrouded his form, and then breathed no more.

His hands fell away from the book.

Arthur had reached out with tentative fingers, and plucked the volume from the grasp of the now-dead hands.

It hadn't been a bible, or a prayer book.

In fact, Arthur realised as he had flicked through its thickened, water-stained pages, he had no idea what it was. Strange diagrams and patterns of letters were mixed in with columns of numbers and, every now and then, a few lines of script, the brown copperplate too small for him to read.

Not a bible then, and not a prayer book. But definitely old, and very possibly valuable.

It was only when he looked up from the book that he noticed the blood.

There was a growing pool of it on the bare, scraped floorboards, spreading out from the old man.

It hadn't been there five minutes ago.

Arthur knew he shouldn't, but before he could stop himself he was pulling back the blanket. He caught a brief glimpse of a chest that appeared to have been caved in by some tremendous weight, and an abdomen that looked as if the contents had not just been torn out but partially eaten before he found himself out on the street with no memory of his frantic flight down the stairs.

It was only the next morning, waking up on a park bench to the scraping caw of crows, that he realised the book had found its way into his pocket.

His first thought was that he would be blamed - both for the priest's murder and for the robbery. Then he remembered how little attention he had been paid both entering and leaving the priest's house, how the few passers-by had failed to acknowledge him, much less give him a second glance.

He spent the first part of the morning trying to get a

look at a newspaper, poking his head into newsagents, leafing through tabloids and broadsheets alike until he was asked to leave. By lunchtime he found himself in the local library. None of the newspapers there had anything about a priest having been found dead of horrific injuries, and by the afternoon he had begun to wonder if he had dreamt the entire episode.

But the book was still there, still nudging his thigh every now and then when he walked, reminding him that it hadn't been a dream, that the book was his now, and that he needed to take better care of it than its last owner.

He stopped outside a pub. What the hell had made him think that?

He looked longingly at the open door, the prospect of the blessed inebriation that lay so close and yet so far away from his penurious grasp almost too much to bear. In fact, so lost was he in his desire for drunken oblivion that he failed to notice the young couple exiting the building. From their over-loud chatter and their general demeanour it was likely that they had entered the pub with the same intention.

He only became aware of them when they walked right into him.

The old man had mumbled his apologies and the girl - young, brash and with the kind of fake tan that looked as if it would peel off if she stood too close to a radiator, muttered something abrasive before giggling and clutching at her partner.

Then they were gone and the old man was alone again, staring at the tiny golden lights flickering behind the pub's mullioned windows. The denial of the promise of warmth, of comfort, of oblivion, was almost too much to bear.

Stop thinking about it, he thought, plunging his hands deep into his pockets. *You haven't got any money, so just stop thinking about it.*

His right hand slid past the book. Its cover felt like stale wet flesh and he grimaced in revulsion at its touch.

There was something beyond it as well. Something deeper inside his pocket. Something bulky yet smooth.

Cautiously, he slid it past that foul volume he no longer wished to touch, and held it in front of him.

It was a woman's purse, made of cheap dark blue plastic.

It felt very full.

He was unable to explain how but he knew it belonged to the girl who had just bumped into him, just as he was unable to explain how, right at that moment, the book was responsible for it being there.

I did that, he felt the book telling him. *I did that, now go in there, have a drink, get comfortable, and read me. And if you don't...*

Of course by the time it had got to that part he was at the bar and collecting the change from a twenty pound note while eyeing what he intended to be the first in a long afternoon of double whiskeys.

He hardly touched it.

It was still there two hours later, sitting on the table in a quiet corner where he had taken it, only occasionally sipped at as the book had rapidly engrossed him.

In the priest's flat he hadn't been able to read it - he was sure of that. But now, as if the veils had fallen away and everything had become clear.

By the time he had left the pub, the whiskey still unfinished, he belonged to the book. It owned him, body and soul. He knew what he had to do, and that the priest had been a warning of what would happen to him if he did not obey. The old man had not needed to be told twice - he had already seen what could happen if the book's instructions were not followed to the letter.

*

And so had begun the long journey that had led him, through the discovery of the sigils, of other documents, of rituals too terrible to bear remembering, to this night, to this most notorious of buildings on an estate with one of the the most horrific reputations in the country.

He looked through the window to his right. Beyond the smears of dirt and bird shit the moon was high now. The time for hesitation and reminiscence was over. The sacrifice of the girl he had made earlier would be in vain if he didn't act now.

He closed his eyes. He was no stranger to pain, but it had always been difficult to inflict it upon himself. A moan escaped his lips as he cut the blade deep across the part of his left wrist just below the thumb, just like in the picture at the back of the book.

Then his eyes were open again and he was directing the steady flow of blood from the severed vein, dripping it slowly to form a circle with himself at its centre. By the time it was complete he was beginning to feel shaky.

Was that a noise from behind him?

He shook his head. It couldn't be - the ritual was nowhere near complete. With a finger dipped in what had already been spilled, he drew an equilateral triangle within the circle, all three points touching the encapsulating rim of red.

There was a clatter as he finished.

It still wasn't time, he thought, and that could only mean one thing.

Someone else was in here with him.

He stared down at his handiwork. He couldn't stop now. He was almost finished. The floor was already beginning to feel weak, pliable, thin.

Thin enough to let something come through.

"What are you doing there?"

The four words were barked harshly and suddenly a white glare brighter than any moonlight was being shone in his eyes. The old man raised his hands and the red running down his arm glistened in the beam from the torch.

"Jesus Christ," said a voice as the light came nearer. "Are you all right?"

No, the old man was not all right, but then neither was the world, he thought as dizziness began to claim him. That was why he had been trying to change it, to give it back to things that were worthier than the tiny, squabbling useless creatures who currently believed themselves to be this planet's masters. Well, he had tried, he thought as his legs gave way. He had tried and failed, but he had come so close. He felt the vague sensation of strong arms dragging him from the circle, smearing his body with the blood he had spilled for the ritual.

All for nothing, he thought. All a failure, as he imagined the floor beginning to undulate softly in his wake.

Little did he realise the night was far from over.

CHAPTER TWO

"The chap in bed one needs an enema. The overdose in bed two needs to throw up. If she hasn't vomited in the next twenty minutes we'd better get out the stomach pump. The drunk in bed three needs to sober up a bit before I can do anything with him, and the weird goth one in bed four I'll get the gynaecologists to take a look at - God knows what she's done with that shampoo bottle but it's well and truly stuck."

Dr Richard Dearden waited in case he needed to repeat any of that, but Staff Nurse Lauren Pike merely gave him a sullen nod and went off to find a couple of sachets of something powerful to instil into the rectum of the unfortunate Mr Johnson. Hopefully that would dislodge the plastic action figure that was uncomfortably obvious on the X-ray, and Richard wouldn't have to refer him to whoever was on for general surgery this evening.

"Look at you! Only five years out of medical school and looking like consultant material already! And how are you getting on, Mr Shiny New A&E Registrar?"

Richard ignored the groan that emanated from behind the closest curtain and gave Julia Chadwick a smile.

"It's only been a week," he said, "but I think I'm getting the hang of it."

"It's good to see you back is what it is," the junior sister replied. "You won't believe some of the people we've had to put up with while we've been waiting for you to come back."

Julia had been a huge help when Richard had worked there as a house officer a couple of years ago. The fact that she was only slightly older than he was had helped them get along, too. She'd been one of the reasons he hadn't minded coming back to Northcote Hospital.

"You're too kind," he said.

"I'm too busy is what I am," she replied. "What are you going to do about the bloke in number five?"

Richard shook his head. "I didn't know there was anyone in there."

Julia handed him an admission card. "Brought in about ten minutes ago. Can't remember his name or date of birth. Can't remember anything very much. Quite a lot of blood on him but only the one laceration." She tapped her hand. "Left wrist, just below the thumb."

Richard raised an eyebrow. "Okay for me to suture or do I need to call vascular?"

"I think you're grown up enough to judge for yourself now, don't you?"

She was right, of course.

"Is he drunk?" Richard asked.

Julia shrugged. "Doesn't smell of alcohol and his pupils aren't dilated. I've taken some bloods. Do you want to add an alcohol level to the tests before I send them off?"

Richard nodded. "Probably should," he said, "just in case. Who brought him in?"

"Security guard up on Northcote Park estate."

Richard's mouth hung open. "You're kidding?"

Julia wasn't. "Apparently the company responsible for tearing Appleton Court down next week is also supposed to make sure no-one gets killed during the demolition. They've had men patrolling the area up there for a couple of weeks now, clearing out the squatters, the drug addicts, and people like this bloke."

Richard glanced at the card. "Self harmer?" he asked.

Julia didn't seem to think so. "More like a no-hoper. Poor bloke. He looks as if he's been living on the street for months, if not years. And be careful when you examine him - pretty much anything you do will make him scream."

Lauren had returned with the enema sachets to try and dislodge Spiderman. The new arrival wasn't the only one who would be screaming soon, Richard thought, as he made his way to bed five.

*

The old man behind the curtain didn't look well.

His eyes were closed, his breathing was rapid despite the oxygen mask, and he could only respond to Richard's questions with vague and unintelligible moans. He was pale and dehydrated, in need of both intravenous fluids and blood. Richard sped up the drip that had been set up in the opposite arm, and checked the admin card to ensure a blood sample had been sent for cross-matching. The patient's heart rate was stable and his blood pressure was slightly low, but hopefully that would come up once they got a bit more saline into him.

Richard pulled on a pair of latex gloves and examined the wound on the man's left wrist. It was superficial, but it was gaping and would need suturing. Richard was careful not to disturb the thick clot that had formed over the lacerated vein. He might need to tie the vessel off, he thought, as he replaced the dressing the paramedics had applied. The man's left shoulder looked awkward as well, and it was tender to examine. That would need to be X-Rayed.

Richard was about to leave to ensure everything had been organised when the man groaned loudly and pointed at a filthy canvas bag that must have been brought in with him.

"Is your medication in there?"

21

If it was that would be a bonus - at least they could find out what the guy was taking, and that would provide a few clues about any chronic illnesses he might have. Richard kept his gloves on and picked the bag up. As he opened it, an odour escaped that reminded him of the waste bins behind the canteen. He held his breath as he rummaged inside.

There were no pill bottles, blister packs, inhalers or injectables. In fact, nothing at all that could be termed therapeutic. The bag contained several weird-looking pieces of jewellery, including a ragged pendant threaded with something that resembled the skull of a tiny monkey, a scuffed ring with a snake emblem, and a number of what looked like dominoes with weird symbols on them.

There was also a small grubby book that made his stomach lurch.

As soon as Richard's fingers brushed against the grim volume the old man nodded and emitted a gurgling noise that could have been interpreted as encouragement. Not that he could see what Richard was touching. Nevertheless, and with some disgust, Richard withdrew the little volume and held it up.

"Is this what you want?" he said in the clear and measured voice that he had found tended to work best with patients who were, to put it kindly, 'a little bit confused.'

The old man's eyes opened slightly. He regarded Richard for a moment before his gaze swung to what Richard was holding in his right hand. Then he began to nod urgently. He reached for it but the drip tethered him, so he tried using his other arm, which caused him to emit an unearthly howl.

"Are you all right behind there?" That was Julia.

"Fine," Richard replied. "I think our new admission has broken his shoulder. We should probably X-Ray his thumb as well before I stitch him up in case the orthopods need to take a look at both."

"I'll let them know."

Richard smiled. Julia was great, and just the kind of person you needed working as a sister down here. The emergency department was right next door to X-Ray, and while he made sure the old guy was okay (he certainly seemed to be perking up) she could pop round and let them know they'd be having a customer in a minute.

It seemed to be the book that had roused the old man from his unconscious state. Now, despite the pain, he was trying to reach for it again.

"All right," Richard said. "Has this got your medical history in it?"

He opened the book at a random page and squinted at the almost illegible, spidery scribblings. Another page showed a picture of a snake, coiled around what looked like a five year old's drawing of the earth. The next two pages boasted a double-page spread of something utterly revolting.

"I don't think you need this right now." Richard put it back into the bag. "We need to get you X-Rayed and stitched up, get some blood inside you, and then you'll start feeling a bit better, all right?"

From the noises his new patient was making, it most certainly was not all right. However, this seemed to be less to do with what Richard had said, and far more about the fact that he had put the book away.

"You can read it later," he said, trying to calm the man down. "It's not going anywhere, and neither are you. Not for the moment."

That didn't seem to help. If anything, it made the man even more agitated.

Richard reached into the bag again and pulled the book

out.

The man visibly calmed.

Richard shrugged and handed it over. If it kept the patient quiet while he was having the X-Rays taken then so much the better, and, after all, what harm could it do? It was probably some kind of self-made bible. Richard had seen a patient once who had claimed to be the sole member of a church he had himself created. That man had written his own bible, too, and when Richard had taken a look it had proved to be as indecipherable as the crumbling tome the old man was now clutching to his chest with his one good hand.

"Is that the bloke for radiology?"

A bullet-shaped head crowned with close-cropped bristling hairs poked round the curtain, the edge gripped by fingers etched with some inexpertly-covered up tattoos.

"Hi Sam." Richard motioned for the porter to come in. "He's all ready to go."

Sam reached over to take the book away from the old man and was rewarded with a snarl.

"That's fine," Richard gave both of them a reassuring smile. "We've agreed that if he behaves himself he can hang onto it." He looked at the old man. "Haven't we?"

Whether or not the old man acknowledged this was difficult to tell, so Richard just let Sam do his job, pushing the trolley bearing his latest patient out of the cubicle and down the corridor towards the X-Ray department.

"Is he fit enough to go?" Julia asked as the trolley brushed past her.

"He's okay," said Richard. "Are his blood results back yet?"

The sister's face looked grim. "That's what I was just coming to tell you about," she said. "It's past ten thirty which means—"

"Oh Christ, yes, I forgot." Richard rolled his eyes.

"The lab technician will have gone home, so either you have to ring up the consultant who then rings him up to get him back in or—"

"I know. Or I go and do it myself." Richard shook his head in exasperation. "What a bloody waste of time."

"It saves the hospital money, apparently," said Julia. "They had someone in to do the calculations and—"

"—and now I have to traipse up to pathology while the patients pile up down here."

Julia gestured to the empty waiting room. "I think we can manage without you for twenty minutes."

A sound, not unlike a large balloon being slowly deflated between two slices of wet liver suddenly came from cubicle one.

"You know what?" Richard tried and failed to suppress a grin. "I think this might be a good time for me to pop out, which is what it sounds like Spiderman is going to do in a minute. I don't think I need to be around for that, do you?"

"Jammy bastard," said Julia, aiming a slap at Richard's behind as he strode smartly away. "The blood samples should be in the lab where the porter left them," she called after him.

There was another horrendous noise from behind her. Sister Julia Chadwick turned round, took a deep breath, and went to see if the action figure Mr Johnson had allegedly sat on had succeeded in managing to do something a spider never would have been able to.

CHAPTER THREE

The darkened corridors of a hospital at night possess their own very special brand of terror.

Like many similar institutions, Northcote Hospital operated a policy of providing only intermittent lighting to the passageways between wards and departments after eleven o'clock at night. Visiting time had been over for two hours, patients had been given their medication and tucked in for the night, and the only souls who now wandered the corridors were those who were expected to know their way in the near-darkness.

Of course, that didn't mean there wasn't the occasional surprise.

It was a curious mixture of patients who sometimes ended up wandering the corridors in the twilight hours. There were the ones with dementia of course, the ones who weren't being watched and were still mobile enough, and quiet enough, to slip out of the ward while the nurse on duty wasn't looking. Searching for friends long gone and lives long past, they haunted the quiet corners until someone was kind enough to lead them back to the psychiatric elderly care ward, where even their addled minds could recognise a friendly face and a warm bed that was apparently theirs.

The addicts were more dangerous.

Actually, Richard thought as he made his way from the emergency department to the service lifts, it was the undiagnosed addicts that were more dangerous, the ones who refused to admit that, unless they had sufficient doses of morphine, or alcohol, or whatever else they had found themselves hooked on. They changed, their desire to obtain whatever they needed swiftly becoming an all-consuming obsession that would allow nothing to stand in its way. This usually meant them setting off the fire alarms as they tried to get out through an emergency exit, or getting themselves worked up into such a state that their snivels and sobs gave away their location to the security guards that had been sent out to find them.

But there were other reasons to be scared as well.

Richard thumbed the button to call one of the service lifts. With any luck it would take him straight to the section in pathology where he needed to go. It also happened to be the same lift where a woman had been stabbed to death by her husband last year. He was in prison, and she was in what the hospital chaplain had termed a 'better place', but it still meant that a lot of staff weren't happy to ride in it.

And fair enough, Richard thought, as the doors slid open and he stepped inside. The tarnished panel boasted buttons with numbers so worn it was almost impossible to read the cracked black plastic. The second up on the right took you to pathology on the fourth floor, and Richard had to push it several times before he had a response. The doors finally slid shut with a creaking protest.

Some people said they'd seen the woman's ghost in the lift.

Of course, they were probably the same people who believed that the government was controlled by aliens (presumably from the planet Stupid, Richard thought with a grin) and that black cats were omens of doom, sent to torment those destined for a horrible death, but that didn't stop him from having to suppress a shiver as the elevator creaked itself upwards. The doors slid open, and Richard tried to ignore any ghostly woman-shaped shadows he might see flickering from the corners of his imagination.

If anything, the fourth floor was even more poorly lit than the ground. Richard stepped out of the lift and tried not to jump when the doors rattled shut behind him. He turned right, then left, aiming for the dim glow at the far end of the corridor. It wasn't until he reached the double doors at the end that he realised he had been holding his breath while he made the trip. His pass card let him through, and he was about to head to where the laboratory analysers were kept when he noticed something odd about the mortuary door.

The room wasn't labelled 'Mortuary'. Hospitals were always very careful about that because of concern that putting a sign over the door might encourage people with what one of Richard's old bosses had politely termed 'unsavoury interests'. Unfortunately, at Northcote Hospital it didn't take much working out because it was the only door in the department that didn't announce its purpose.

And despite the time getting on for midnight, it looked as if there was a light on inside.

He could ignore it, he thought. But what if someone had got trapped in there? What if someone had tripped and hit their head four hours earlier, and now they were slowly freezing to death? What if they were discovered tomorrow morning and he knew he could have helped them? What would happen when someone realised that his security pass had been used up here, and then everyone else found out that he could have helped them?

For Christ's sake open the fucking door, he told himself. *Even if it's zombies it'll be better than the night of torment and guilt you seem to be trying to give yourself right now.*

It swung open at his touch.

Nearly blinded by the fluorescent tube lighting, Richard had put his hand in front of his eyes when a voice called out,

"What do you want?"

The door to the post mortem room was open, and as his eyes began to adjust Richard could see a figure moving about in there. He was sure he recognised the voice, but it was only when the figure poked his head out that he realised who it was.

"Dev!" Richard tried not to sound too relieved. "What the hell are you doing here so late?"

Dr Dev Choudry wiped his hands on the green plastic apron that was protecting his clothes from the fall out from his latest autopsy. "Too much work and not enough hours in the day," the pathologist said, shaking his head. "But at least the hospital has agreed to pay me overtime. What brings you up to the land of the no-longer-living?"

Richard gestured behind him with his thumb. "I need to use the blood analysers," he said.

Dev nodded. "Oh yeah," he said. "I saw the email that went round about that. You know, I don't think they should be letting just anyone operate that equipment. It's expensive, and before you know it some trainee will have squirted the wrong thing into the wrong chamber and everything will be out of operation for a week."

"Yes," said Richard. "I am rather counting on there being instructions on the side of the machine for me to follow."

Dev raised his eyebrows. "Are you being serious?"

Actually, Richard was. "I don't suppose you know how to work it, do you?" he asked.

"Come with me," Dev sighed, peeling off his gloves and demonstrating an expert aim at a faraway bin.

"Looks like you get a lot of practice at that," said Richard with a grin.

"If I miss, I have to clean the floor," Dev replied. "So it helps me concentrate."

"You're sure I'm not disturbing you?"

"I'm sure you *are* disturbing me." Dev returned his smile. "But to be honest I could do with a break."

Richard looked over his shoulder. On the table in the post mortem room, he could see the opened-up specimen of a young woman.

"Can't the dead wait until morning anymore?" he asked.

"The dead can," said Dev, "but the Coroner's Office is another matter. It's all very hush hush at the moment so you need to keep this to yourself. That girl in there was found on the outskirts of Northcote Park estate earlier today. I'm not sure what the rush is but they wanted the PM doing right away. Some fuss about a possible ritual slaying. Not that I've got any experience with that sort of thing. "

"Well you've certainly got stuck in," said Richard, eyeing the ragged open chest cavity and the jaw that had been detached from the face.

"I haven't got started yet," Dev said. "That's how they found her."

An involuntary chill swept through Richard's insides.

"Come on," said the pathologist, "I'll show you how to operate the blood analysers. Then you're on your own. And if you make a mess I'll know who to blame."

*

It was actually quite easy, but then most lab tests were once you'd been shown how to do them, Richard thought as he watched Dev pipette tiny drops of the old man's blood from the glass tubes he had filled down in the emergency department.

"Are you going to need the samples for anything else?"

Richard shook his head. "I don't think so."

Dev was about to push the half-full sample bottles into one of the bright yellow SharpSafe containers lined up against the wall when Richard stopped him.

"Actually," he said, "let's hang onto them for the moment. I'm not really sure what's wrong with him and I don't want to have to go sticking him again unless I really have to."

"In that case, you'll have to take them back down to the emergency department."

Richard frowned. "Aren't they supposed to be stored up here?" he asked.

"Should be," Dev nodded. He pointed to a huge white refrigeration unit that took up one entire corner of the lab. "But there's no room. If you want to keep them you'll have to find somewhere downstairs to store them."

"Any interesting results?" Richard was double-bagging the tubes prior to putting them in his pocket.

Dev said nothing.

"Are they not through yet? I thought these machines were supposed to be fast!"

"They are," Dev said, giving Richard a sober look. "I think you'd better get back to your chap. According to these results he should already be dead."

"You mean he's really ill?"

Dev pointed at the print out on the screen. "I mean he's dead. He's so anaemic he doesn't have enough blood to carry oxygen around his system. His electrolytes are so up the spout his heart should have stopped, and his kidneys probably haven't worked for a week." The pathologist narrowed his eyes. "This isn't some kind of joke, is it?"

Richard shook his head again. "Maybe I've brought up the wrong bloods," he said.

Dev waved a piece of green paper in front of Richard's face. "Isn't this your handwriting on the request forms?"

"Yes." Richard looked stumped. "Perhaps something

happened to the samples on the way up? Some contamination already in the collection tubes? Or perhaps I made some mistake taking them?"

Dev raised his eyebrows. "And in your opinion, Dr Dearden, how many blood samples have you taken during your long and illustrious career?"

"Thousands," Richard admitted. "The mistake isn't there. If there is a mistake at all."

"Like I said." Dev rose from his chair, obviously intending to get back to work, "you'd better go and see how your patient is doing. Or not doing, as the case may be."

"I will," Richard nodded, grateful to have something to distract him from the unsettling trip back down to the emergency department.

"Let me know if he's still moving," Dev said. "It could make an interesting case report."

By the time Richard had reached the lifts and was pressing the button he could hear the pathologist calling after him. "And if you do write it up, make sure you put my name on it!"

But by the time Richard had got back to the emergency department, the old man had vanished.

CHAPTER FOUR

"Where's he gone?" Richard gazed at the empty cubicle in disbelief. Everything was gone - the patient, the trolley he had been lying on, even the monitoring equipment he had been attached to.

"Orthopaedics," said a voice from behind him.

Richard turned to confront Julia. "Already?" he said. "Why?"

"Simple," said the sister. "He came back from X-Ray and it was obvious from the pictures that he'd broken his shoulder. The orthopaedic registrar just happened to still be here fixing a Colles' fracture so I passed the films over to her. She arranged for him to be admitted onto one of their wards and the porters were free to take him, so he went." Julia snapped her fingers. "Just like that."

"But his blood test results are all over the place!" Richard persisted.

"His blood test results are no longer your responsibility." Julia's voice was firm.

"Well, can we store these somewhere anyway?" Richard handed over the blood samples.

"All right," said Julia, sounding as if it wasn't all right at all. "Seeing as it's you."

When she returned Richard asked which ward the old man had been taken to.

Julia shook her head. "Why should you be bothered? You've got another half an hour to go on your shift and then you're out of here. If you really want to find out what happened to him then by all means do it on your own time, but right now you have patients waiting."

There was nothing Richard could do, other than spend the next thirty minutes reviewing the drug overdose (who thankfully had vomited and now just needed referral to the physicians), seeing an eighty seven year old lady with a hip fracture (Off to orthopaedics for you, Richard thought, remembering to ask about his other 'referral' of the evening while he was on the phone), and checking on Mr Johnson. Spiderman was proving resilient and so it was with a stifled smile that he rang up Barney Williams.

"You're on for general surgery tonight, aren't you Barney?"

"Yes." The voice on the other end of the phone was hesitant. Barney hated being disturbed anytime after ten o'clock because that was when his wife went to bed and he could settle down to watch some of the terrible films he enjoyed.

"I'm afraid I've got a foreign body wedged in the rectum for you."

There was a pause, then, "Has no-one explained to you the fruit is supposed to go in the other end?"

Richard laughed. "My own personal habits are none of your business my friend, unless of course I go a bit too far, which is what our Mr Johnson has done." Richard pulled up the X-Ray and squinted at it. "What we have here is a forty-five year old man with what looks like a six-inch-high action figure jammed several inches inside his back passage. We've tried enemas and laxatives but no luck."

There was a groan from the other end. "The problem with those is they can perforate the bowel if you leave them in for too long," said Barney. "I'll need to take him to theatre. Can you ring Eleanor. She's my house officer on tonight and she can get him sorted while I come in."

"Sure." Richard was about to put the phone down. "What film were you watching?"

A pause. *"The Unbearable Lightness of Being."*

"Bollocks."

"Oh all right then, *The Blood Spattered Bride.*"

"That sounds more like it," Richard chuckled. "I'll have finished my shift by the time you get here so good luck with getting it out."

"Who is it by the way?"

"The action figure?" Richard squinted at the X-Ray again. "It's difficult to tell, but according to the patient it's Spiderman."

"Peter Parker would have been ashamed."

"But J Jonah Jameson would have given it front page coverage. You can tell me all about it tomorrow."

"You mean later today!"

Do I? thought Richard, as he put the receiver down and looked at the clock.

Ten past midnight.

"That's me out of here," he said to everyone, grabbing his coat.

"Me too," said Julia, chasing after him. "Do you need a lift home?

Richard shook his head. "I've got my car. Besides, I need to pop up to the ward and see how that old bloke's doing."

"You really don't, you know," said the sister. "What you need is a nice cup of cocoa and a good tucking in."

Richard beamed from ear to ear. "You know I can't stand cocoa."

"But I can guarantee you'd love the tucking in," she said with a mischievous smile. "We can keep the cocoa optional."

"Sadly, we have to make the entire thing optional tonight," Richard replied.

They walked out of the department together. To Richard, the corridor seemed even darker than earlier.

"Is a bloke with a broken shoulder really more interesting than me?" Julia asked him.

Richard shook his head. "It's not his shoulder. It's him. The blood results Dev Choudry got out of the machine were incompatible with life."

Julia shrugged. "Well he should know all about that. What was he doing here so late?"

"Horrible murder that they wanted him to look at. I've probably already said too much."

Julia narrowed her eyes. "Really?"

Richard nodded. "Yes, really. In fact I wouldn't be surprised if Dev is still up there."

They had reached the main entrance to the hospital. The glass doors slid apart invitingly just as Julia made to slip between them.

"If you're not too late you could still drop by," she said by way of farewell.

"Not tonight."

"But sometime?"

Richard gave her a 'don't tempt me' expression and laid a gentle hand on her shoulder. "Aren't you supposed to be getting back together with that husband of yours?"

Julia shrugged. "We've both promised to try again, but you can't blame a girl for exploring her options."

Richard brushed his lips against her forehead. "You take

care," he said, "and I'll see you on your next shift."

They waved each other goodbye. Richard waited outside until Julia was across the parking lot and safely at her car, the image of the torn-apart girl on Dev's dissection table still strong in his mind.

Then he went back into the building to find where that old man had got to.

And to see if he was still alive.

CHAPTER FIVE

Arthur Lipscomb's eyes flickered open.

He looked at the side room to which he had been transferred through narrow, crusted eyelids, his blurred vision gradually resolving to take in the dimly lit surroundings. To his left, the heart monitor he had been wired up to beeped regularly. To his right, a window allowed him a view from the third floor room out over the city. If he craned his neck he could see Appleton Court, a dark and impassive monolith on the city skyline.

Perhaps all was not yet lost.

If he turned his head the other way he could just see the sign that had been placed above and to the left of his bed. The red letters on a white background were big enough for him to read, even from this angle. 'Nil By Mouth', the sign said. He vaguely remembered something one of the doctors had said about him needing his shoulder fixed. They had also taken yet more blood from him, explaining that there must have been a problem with the analyser the first time.

Arthur knew there wasn't a problem with their machines. The results would come back the same when the tests were rechecked. He was living on borrowed time, as he had been for the last couple of months.

And there was still so much to do.

At least they had been able to work out his blood type, he thought, as he regarded the cannula emerging from his right wrist. His eyes followed the scarlet pipe that led to the bag of blood raised high above his head. Good, he thought, they had given him something he could use.

He disconnected the heart monitor, taking care to press

the large button that was helpfully labelled 'Silence Alarm', and then gripped the mattress with his good hand. At first his fingers had difficulty finding purchase on the bed sheet and it slid over the rubber coated mattress beneath, but eventually he was able to pull himself into a sitting position.

Now to get out of the bed.

Ignoring the biting pain of his left shoulder, the old man shuffled as far as he could to the right side of the mattress. Then, keeping his mouth tightly shut to suppress his cries of pain, he swung himself so that his legs dangled over the side.

So far so good.

It was when he tried to stand up that he ran into problems.

His left ankle, the one with the growth erupting from its outer aspect, gave way as soon as he tried to put weight on it. Falling forwards, he tried to steady himself by grabbing at the table that had been placed by the bedside. Under the pressure of his weight, and with the aid of the wheels that all such pieces of hospital furniture come equipped with, the table careered towards the window and the old man went with it. His crash to the floor was accompanied by a disquieting crack of a number of diseased joints.

Biting back howls of pain, the old man looked to his right. The network of tubing that until a moment ago had been delivering blood to his right arm had become disconnected, and now the life-giving plasma was being drip-fed onto the jaundiced linoleum of the floor.

There was no time to lose.

He pulled himself to his feet, gently testing his ankle and finding to his relief that it was more likely sprained than broken. Bracing himself against the mattress, and using his right foot to get it moving, he pushed the bed over to the wall opposite the window.

After pausing for a moment to catch his breath, he lifted the blood bag down from its stand and, taking hold of the still-dripping giving set in his right hand, began to draw the same pattern he had begun up at Appleton Court. He smiled as he worked. It was much easier doing this with blood that wasn't dripping from a self-inflicted wound, and after all, the blood was ostensibly his, even if it hadn't actually been transfused into his own body. Surely the powers he was trying to call into this dimension would understand that?

Once the geometric shapes had been drawn, he pinched the plastic tube to shut off the flow of blood, and struggled over to the cheap plywood wardrobe. It was so dark inside he could barely see, and as he rummaged around he felt a brief a moment of panic before his fingers settled around the clasp of his bag. He pulled it out and tipped its contents of bones, amulets and tiny carved stone figures onto the floor.

Then he opened the book.

The diagram he needed was close to the end. The book refused to stay open while he worked and so, knowing that if he delayed now he may not live to try again and all would be lost, he ripped out the necessary page. It came loose from its bindings with ease, almost as if that had been the intention all along. The old man tore free the surgical tape that had been used to secure the cannula to the vein in his arm, and used it to fix the loose page to the wall beneath the window, so that he could see both it and the looming outline of Appleton Court as he worked. With infinite care he reproduced, in blood, the symbols detailed on the yellow parchment. He knew it wasn't just the complex sigils he was drawing that were important, but also the spaces around them. If the entire diagram wasn't drawn perfectly, the ritual would not work.

There were only a few drops left in the transfusion bag by the time he had finished.

Breathing rapidly, his weak heart beating a thready

tattoo against his osteoporotic breastbone, the old man now began to arrange the sacred objects at prescribed points in and around the circle, again taking care to position them exactly as the book described. Once he had finished he leaned against the bed once more, panting. Moonlight was now streaming through the window. A thin sheen of sweat caused the unhealthy flesh of his arms to shine with a greasy pallor.

Almost time.

Once the old man had his breath back he picked up the book. The fleshy cover felt as moist as his own skin. He held it up in front of his face and, just for a moment, fancied he could almost see it breathing.

Then he turned to the page that held the incantation.

*

"I'm about to fix a hip, Richard, is this urgent?"

The orthopaedic registrar's name was Sandra Harris. She was at the end of her training scheme and was due to become a consultant later in the year. Right now, she sounded at the end of her tether as well.

Richard held the telephone receiver away from his ear to avoid being deafened by her voice. "It's about that chap you admitted from casualty," he said.

"Which one?" There was a sigh and the sound of rustling paper as a list was presumably examined. "There have been so many in tonight I've lost count. As usual."

"Old guy, fractured left shoulder." Richard tried to think of anything else that might help. "We weren't able to ascertain his name or date of birth so those details might be listed as unknown."

Another, more exasperated sigh emanated from the receiver.

"We don't admit patients without details, Richard. I

would have thought even you knew that."

Richard tried not to shout. "Well someone must have found them out, then, because he's definitely gone somewhere."

"Hang on," said Sandra. "I'll have a word with Simon, my house officer."

Richard held the receiver further away again as Sandra shouted across the echoing chamber of the orthopaedic operating theatre. He could just make out a young man's mumbled reply but it was impossible to understand what he said. Then Sandra was talking to him again.

"Sorry Richard," she said. "I'd forgotten all about that guy. It's been bloody awful up here all night. Julia rang me with that one, keen to offload him - waiting times and all that —" Richard nodded - the hospital's prescribed targets on waiting times in the emergency department were known for causing huge headaches amongst the teams patients got referred to. "Anyway, it sounded like he'd be coming to us eventually so I just said yes and planned to see him later." Richard heard her shouting at Simon again and yet another cowed response.

"Simon says he admitted him on to Yew Tree Ward. Apparently there was some concern about him being an infection risk?"

"Not especially from my point of view," Richard replied. "But he did look rather unkempt."

"Well, Simon put him in a side room anyway, just to be on the safe side."

A side room on Yew Tree. Richard should be able to find that fairly easily. "Did Simon look at his blood results?

There was more shouting, more mumbling, and then some screaming from Sandra.

"Sorry about that Richard," she said when the noise had

died down. "Simon says he got some blood cross-matched for the guy but the other results were so out of whack he did them again. But he never told me. Is he unstable?"

More like nearly dead, Richard thought. "His electrolytes were completely up the spout and his haemoglobin was so low you can probably count the red cells floating through his arteries by hand."

Now there were more voices muttering in the background.

"Richard I've got to go - the patient's on the table."

"Sure." Richard looked at his watch. It was well past his shift but he couldn't leave things like this. "Do you want me to pop up to the ward and make sure he's ok?"

It was rare for anyone to hear the tones of Sandra Harris, orthopaedic surgeon, soften and sound grateful, but now Richard could count himself among the privileged few.

"That would be so brilliant if you could, Richard. Has casualty suddenly calmed down or something?"

"I'm off shift," he admitted. "Juan Velasquez is down there now. I was about to go home."

"In that case I really owe you. Thanks ever so much."

"Just one final thing," Richard took out his pen.

"What?"

"You haven't told me his name."

Another scream, another shout, another mumble.

"At least Simon managed to get that much out of him," came the reply. "His name is Lipscomb, Richard. Arthur Lipscomb."

*

The old man in the side room on Yew Tree ward often

had trouble remembering his name. It had been so long since anyone had used it that it had taken him a while to recall it. The young man with the stethoscope draped around his neck who had come to see him in this room had smiled and written it on a piece of paper. He had asked a few more questions that Arthur couldn't answer, taken another blood test, and gone away. Almost as soon as he had left a nurse had come in, called him by his name several times, checked his temperature, and then put the sign above his bed. Then she had gone away too, only to return with the bag of blood and a younger, prettier nurse to help her. They had both called him Arthur as they had connected up the life-giving fluid, and given him smiles that made him think they were probably very nice people. So was that young doctor, and the others who had seen him in the emergency department downstairs. All of them, all such nice people.

But they were all going to die.

The book breathed again, expanding and contracting slightly against his quivering fingers.

"I know." His voice was little more than a croaking whisper. "I know. We're both eager to see this begun, you and I. Both so eager…"

And with that he began to read aloud. Words in a language unheard in aeons. From deep within his throat he pronounced the series of clashed consonants and strings of diphthongs, accenting and enunciating the awful-sounding syllables in the way he had been practising these past few months. Practicing deliberately and oh-so-carefully - only one tiny fragment a day, and absolutely not in the sequence they were laid down here, lest he have to suffer the consequences of an inappropriate and ill-timed meeting of universes.

As he finished the first page he thought he heard a creaking noise coming from beneath him.

He paused.

After a few seconds of silence it happened again. The sound was almost imperceptible, but it was definitely there. Anyone else would have attributed it to someone moving something heavy on the floor below, but Arthur Lipscomb knew different.

The sounds weren't coming from the next floor down.

They were coming from the floor itself.

Or rather, from that part of a different and terrible dimension that was trying to replace the structure beneath his feet, the structure beneath the circle and the intricate symbols he had drawn in blood.

He was about to turn the page when the book suddenly expanded and then, just as quickly, contracted in his grasp. The volume fell from his trembling fingers almost as if it knew what was about to happen, and was taking a deep breath to steady itself for the horrors to come. It landed on the floor with the wet, slapping sound of a saturated sponge.

When he reached down to pick the book up, the floor moved.

Just like the sound he had heard, the movement was slight, and anyone not looking for it could have been forgiven for missing it. But now there was a slight upward curve to the previously flat surface, centred around the middle of the circle he had drawn.

He blinked once, twice, and then the scuffed tiles resumed their former shape.

The book had breathed, the floor had breathed, and now it was Arthur Lipscomb's turn to take a halting gasp of air. His chest rattled as he inhaled more deeply than he had in weeks, opening up parts of his lungs that had not been used since he was much younger. His bronchioles protested, the tiny tubes unsticking themselves with a pleuritic pain that caused multiple pin-point agonies throughout his ribcage. He coughed, bringing up tiny drops of blood that speckled the circle and threatened to alter the appearance of some of the sigils he had marked within it.

There wasn't much time.

He cleared his throat, swallowed what had come into his mouth as a result, and began the next stage of the incantation.

As he spoke the words, the floor began to move again, rising and falling rhythmically like the bellowed lungs of some enormous beast. With each completed phrase the movements grew greater, until he was in danger of becoming overbalanced.

He found himself fighting nausea as well as the pain in his chest, shoulder and ankle. Blood dribbles down his chin as he read aloud the final passage that would complete the book's long-made plans.

As the last word left his lips the floor, stretched to breaking point, suddenly burst open.

Arthur Lipscomb, bleeding and in pain, could only stare in silent horror at the thing that had come through the rent to claim him.

It was only then that he realised he had made a terrible mistake

*

"And you are?"

Richard flashed his ID at the nurse sitting at the duty desk on Yew Tree ward. The badge attached to the right breast pocket of the white uniform stretched tight over her ample bulges identified her as Health Care Auxiliary Kerry Morris.

"I'm looking for Arthur Lipscomb," he said, slightly out of breath from climbing the stairs. Both service lifts to this part of the floor had been busy and he hadn't wanted to wait.

Kerry turned around, her swivel chair protesting as she did, and squinted at the whiteboard on the wall behind her.

"He's not here," she said after what seemed like an age.

"Mr Hampton's registrar said she'd had him admitted here," Richard persisted.

Kerry shook her head. "Haven't seen her all evening."

Richard sighed. "She couldn't come to see him herself," he said. "She sent Simon the house officer up."

Kerry's eyes brightened at that. "Ooo yes, I like him," she said, a little more animatedly.

Never mind about that, Richard thought. "Simon clerked him in one of your side rooms, apparently." What else could he say to stir her into sluggish action? "He's probably having a blood transfusion?"

The girl tried to think. It was a long and painful process and Richard resisted the urge to look at his watch for fear of distracting her.

"I think there's someone having some blood in side room one," she said eventually.

Thank God, thought Richard.

"But that's a woman. Hip replacement for tomorrow, I think."

Richard was seriously considering searching every room himself (except side room one, probably) when there was a crash from behind him.

From side room four.

"Who's in there?" he asked.

Kerry looked at the board and frowned.

"No-one," she said. "The box is empty."

"You mean nobody's filled it in," said Richard. "Would you mind if I went and had a look?"

But Kerry was already ignoring him and tapping at the computer keyboard in front of her. She frowned and bit her lip as she repeatedly hit the return button.

"Computer's gone down again." She gave Richard a look he could only describe as bovine.

There was another crash, followed by an ear-splitting scream.

"I think I'll just pop along and see what's going on," Richard said, and then added, almost as an afterthought. "You'd better call security."

Kerry frowned. "Why?"

"In case that's not Mr Lipscomb having a funny turn." Richard was already on his way to side room four. The door was closed and as he went to open it he found himself jerking his hand back.

The door handle was hot.

That was ridiculous, he thought, and tried again.

No. It was definitely searingly, pain-inducingly, bloody hot.

Before he knew it, and with astonishing speed he would never have thought her capable of, Kerry was beside him.

"Ow!" She yelped as she tried to open the door.

"I know," Richard nodded. "Weird, isn't it?"

"He was weird when they brought him in," Kerry said, still staring at the door handle while nursing her hand. "Mumbling all that weird stuff. I didn't realise they were going to put him here. Simon said he was going to get the psychiatrists to see him in the morning."

"What did you think?"

Kerry shook her head. "There's no way you'd get the psychiatrists to see anyone quicker than a week," she said. "They always take bloody ages to come."

"Not them," Richard said. "Him. Did you think he was off his rocker?"

The girl smiled for the first time since Richard had met her. It was actually very nice. "Completely barmy," she said. "Rambling about gods and monsters and parallel universes. I thought I was in the X Files for a minute."

We might still be, Richard thought, and then told himself not to be so stupid.

A sound like a car being twisted in the hands of a giant caused the door to rattle.

"I don't want to go in there," Kerry said.

Neither do I, thought Richard. He took out his handkerchief and wrapped it around his right hand. "You go and get security," he said. "I'm going to find out what's happening in there."

When he looked again she was gone.

Probably very sensible, he thought, as he grabbed the shaking handle and flung the door open to see what had become of Arthur Lipscomb.

CHAPTER SIX

Richard blinked.

There was no-one in the room.

As soon as the door had opened the rattling had ceased, the noise had stopped, and now the door handle was no longer hot.

The room, however, was a bloody mess.

Someone had pushed the bed up against the near wall. The better part of the contents of a blood bag had been used to draw a circle on the floor, as well as some weird symbols inside it. Richard peered at the images. One or two were now so smudged that, if they had ever been legible they certainly weren't now. The rest were like nothing he had ever seen before. The curtains had been drawn back and the moon shone on the smeared design, as if to say 'Here! Here is where all that noise was coming from! It may not look like it now but believe me it was! I should know - I saw it all!'

Although he had no desire to, Richard took a step inside. The floor felt strange. It squished slightly underfoot as if the tiles were made of fungus. He resisted the urge to crouch down and test the theory with his fingers.

At the end of the bed were the occupant's drug chart and observation records. Richard grabbed the bright blue folder and flipped it open, relieved to come across something from the normal world in a room that felt as if it had suddenly become a part of something else entirely. The details at the front confirmed that the patient who should have been in the empty bed was Arthur Lipscomb. He was supposed to be receiving a blood transfusion, and had been written up for painkillers.

But where was he?

Richard sniffed the air. As well as the usual hospital odours of antiseptic and other, more natural, human aromas, he could smell something else. Something gritty and metallic, sulphur mixed with ozone. It had been stronger when he had entered the room but now it was fading.

There was nothing to explain what had caused the noise.

Richard turned on all the lights in the room and looked under the bed, just in case.

Nothing.

The room was empty apart from the bed, a blood bag, some charts, and a weird picture on the floor.

And that book, the one the old man had been making such a fuss about in the emergency department.

Richard hadn't spotted it at first as it was lying face down, its cover the same drained flesh colour as the floor tiles. Richard had crouched and was about to pick it up when he was interrupted by a voice from the door.

"Is everything all right in here, doctor?"

Richard turned to see Steve Parkyn, one of the security guards, poking his friendly face around the door.

"One of our patients has gone walkabout," said Richard, getting to his feet.

"Looks like he made a right mess before he did," said Steve as he surveyed the room.

"And a right old noise as well." That was Kerry from behind him.

"Nurse!" An elderly female voice was calling from one of the ward bays. "What's all the noise about?"

"Nothing to worry about, Mrs Jeffries." Kerry went off to

reassure the old lady, as well as anyone else on the ward who had been woken by the disruption.

"Is that the truth?" Steve whispered once she had gone.

"What?"

"That there's nothing to worry about."

"I really don't know, Steve." Richard gestured around him. "Look at all of this."

Steve whistled. "Looks like something out of Dennis Wheatley if you ask me," he said.

"Dennis who?"

"Before your time, young sir. These days it's all *Harry Potter* and *Lord of the Rings,* but back when I was a lad the popular stuff to read was *The Devil Rides Out* and *To the Devil A Daughter* - you know, all that black magic stuff."

Richard flashed him a grin. "They had *Lord of the Rings* in your day, Steve."

"That they did," said Steve, "but you didn't read that in the playground unless you wanted to get your glasses stamped on."

Fair enough. "So you think our missing patient's been practising witchcraft?"

Steve shrugged. "Absolutely no bloody idea, but if something were to pop up looking like Christopher Lee it wouldn't surprise me one bit."

"Mr Lipscomb actually looks more like a worn-out Gandalf." Richard plunged his hands into his pockets and sighed. "Wherever he might be now."

"Is that blood?" Steve was looking at the circle.

"I think so."

"Have you got your phone on you?"

Richard nodded. "Why?"

"If I were you, I'd take a picture of that. Just in case it might be helpful to find your chap. I can't imagine that nurse is going to let this room stay in this sort of state for long. Once you're gone that'll all be mopped up."

He was right, of course. Richard took shots from various angles and included a few of the room for good measure.

"I'll get the rest of the lads to keep an eye out for him," Steve said. "Kenny's on the CC TV tonight. I'm guessing he hasn't spotted anything or I'd already know, but I'll run a check on the tapes for the last half an hour or so, just to make sure."

"Cheers, Steve." Richard was dying to take a look at the book but it was important the search got underway for Mr Lipscomb. He waved the phone in the air. "Let me know if you have any luck."

"Same here," said Steve. His radio crackled to signify that someone was trying to get hold of him. "I'll get to work. Do you want me to close this door? We don't want any of these old dears looking in and having a heart attack, do we?"

"You better had," Richard said with a weak smile. "After all, who knows how many Dennis Wheatley fans there are on the ward at the moment?"

As soon as Steve had shut the door, Richard wished he hadn't. There was something wrong in here. Something cloying and insidious. He could feel it pressing around him, trying to constrict his chest, creep up his nose and fill his lungs with its strangeness.

Get out of there, then.

He would, Richard promised himself, just as soon as he picked up that book.

It felt fleshy and spongy and seemed to contract slightly

when his fingers made contact with it, almost as if it was trying to get away from him.

There was something strange underneath it.

Inexplicably glad to put it back down, Richard laid the book aside and peered at what he had uncovered. At first glance it looked like an irregularity on one of the floor tiles. He brushed his fingers across it.

Bumps.

Tiny half-moon-shaped bumps.

Four of them.

Like fingernails.

Because that was the most likely explanation for where Arthur Lipscomb had gone, wasn't it? He'd somehow been sucked into the floor and merged with the floor tiles. Or perhaps he'd melted into them? Richard shook his head. This place really was starting to get to him if he was starting to imagine nonsense like that. He picked up the book again and flicked through it. It felt alien, and the paper seemed to stick to his fingers, almost as if the book wanted him to look at certain pages.

Put it down.

He couldn't, though. The weird spider-like scribbles and strange diagrams were oddly compelling, so much so in fact that Richard found himself trying to pronounce some of the words.

The light in the room flickered, and darkened.

Stop reading, he told himself.

But it was no use.

Richard spoke another word and a foetid breeze stung his nostrils.

Something was behind him.

Something much bigger than he was.

Something huge, in fact

With a gasp of horror he realised it was the stinking breath of this titan that was violating the air around him.

Frozen to the spot, Richard tried to tear his eyes from the book, tried to stop himself from reading out any more of the arcane passage that he was somehow being compelled to, knowing that one more word, even one more syllable, could mean his doom.

The door to the side room opened with a bang and Kerry poked her head in.

"Can I get this place cleaned up now?" she said in the loudest, most abrasive, most wonderful tones Richard had ever heard. The hold the book had over him was instantly broken, and so he snapped it shut and stuffed it into his pocket. At least he could stop anyone else from finding it and coming under its spell.

He mumbled something to Kerry that he hoped made sense, and then dragged himself out of there, out of that room where something horrible had happened, something otherworldly, something no-one should ever have to know about.

Something he was now sure had almost happened to him.

*

"Are you still here?" Dev Choudry looked at the clock above the mortuary door before checking his own watch to make sure it was right. "It's almost one o'clock in the morning!"

"I know." It was all Richard was able to mumble as he slumped onto a chair near the door.

Dev put down his scalpel and moved back from the half-dissected body of the girl on the table. "Are you all right?"

Richard shook his head. "It's turning into a very weird night," he said.

"It must be if you haven't gone home yet." Dev gestured to the book his friend was holding in his right hand. "What's that?"

"Something weird." Richard got back on his feet. "I was actually wondering if you might take a look at it."

Dev snorted. "Why? I don't know anything about books."

"No." Richard dropped it onto the stainless steel work bench, taking care not to disturb the body Dev had been working on. It landed with a wet thump. "But you know about human flesh, and I think that's what this might be made of."

He was rewarded with a mirthless laugh. "Richard, it's bloody late. I've got to write up my report on this girl and then get to bed so I can be back here for seven am to look at a load of breast biopsies. I haven't got time to piss about."

"I know." Richard wondered how much he should tell Dev, how much his friend would believe, and most importantly how likely it would be that he would call the psychiatrists and get Richard committed for the night. "I just witnessed something very weird, and I think this book has something to do with it."

Despite the lateness of the hour and his drooping eyelids, Dev looked intrigued. "How weird?"

"A man disappeared from his side room. No, that isn't right. I think a man might have been sucked into the floor of his side room, after he'd drawn some weird patterns on the floor that Steve from security said looked like devil worship stuff. Then when I opened that book I could swear something materialised behind me. Something that wanted to kill me."

Dev was obviously having difficulty keeping the

incredulous grin off his face. "And the weird bit in there is...?"

"All of it!" Richard could tell he wasn't getting anywhere. "You weren't there," he said. "You didn't see it."

"Neither did you by the sound if it." Dev clearly wasn't impressed. "A man who wasn't there and something you felt was behind you but which I'm guessing you didn't see?" Richard was forced to nod. It did sound ridiculous when Dev put it like that. "I think you've been worn out by this place even more than I have," said the pathologist. "Get home, get some shiraz inside you, and get to sleep."

The prospect of bed suddenly seemed extremely inviting.

"You're probably right." Richard rubbed his eyes. "Sorry to bother you, Dev."

"Don't mention it," said the pathologist with a tired smile. "And don't forget your book."

Richard reached for it And the body on the table between them emitted a load groan.

Richard looked at Dev as he backed away. "I didn't imagine that, did I?"

Dev shook his head as yet another wet bubbling sound came from the opened throat of the post mortem specimen.

Then her eyes opened.

Dev picked up the scalpel and backed away. "Richard, what the hell is going on?"

"I don't know," Richard replied, as the ravaged, eviscerated girl turned her half-dissected face first to Dev, and then to him.

When she spotted the book lying beside her, her lipless mouth turned into a rictus grin.

"She shouldn't be doing that!" A panicked Dev was echoing Richard's sentiments exactly but Richard didn't appear to be listening. The thing on the autopsy table was pushing itself into a sitting position, and what remained of the girl's heart and lungs fell from her chest cavity, onto her bloodstained thighs. She regarded her own innards for a moment, her once pretty face creasing with confusion, before ragged fingers reached for the book beside her.

"We mustn't let her get it!" Richard cried. The girl clutched at the fleshy tome, but he was too quick and knocked it to the floor.

The girl's face transformed into an expression of anger as, with jerky, awkward movements, she dragged herself from the table and stood before him, a twitching, rasping, undead thing of horror.

"What should I do?" Richard shouted to Dev over the thing's shoulder.

"How the hell should I know?"

"Because she's your bloody corpse, that's why!"

The girl took a step forward.

"She never moved a muscle until you came in!"

Another step.

"Well she's bloody well moving now, isn't she?"

The girl craned her head a little, and twisted her neck from side to side, almost as if she was sniffing the air. Then she looked down to where the book had fallen.

"I think that's what she wants," Dev said, moving round to the girl's left side.

"Well why don't we let her have it then?" Richard had stopped, but only because there was a wall to prevent him from backing away any further.

"When is it ever a good idea to let a living corpse have a book that you've already said is satanic?"

"I didn't say that - Steve the security guard did."

"Never mind who said it." Dev was crouching now. "Kick it away from her!"

This was not the time for Richard to realise he was rooted to the spot.

"I can't move!"

The girl was trying to bend down now, threads of muscle hanging from her outstretched right arm as she tried to reach for the book.

"Yes you can!" Dev shouted. "If you don't we're probably not going to make it out of here."

Richard took a deep breath and tried to ignore the odour of toxic chemicals and raw flesh that filled his nostrils. With strength borne of desperation he shoved himself away from the wall. He dived to the floor, grabbed the book, and threw it to Dev.

The girl hissed in frustration.

"Don't give it to me!" Dev cried as the thing staggered around the autopsy table towards him.

"What else am I supposed to do?"

The corpse was almost on him when Dev threw the book back to Richard.

The girl began to make her way back to the door.

"We can't keep doing this all night!" Richard shouted as he began to back away once more.

"Hang on." Dev was searching for something. "Keep her occupied for a minute."

"How the hell am I supposed to do that?" Richard kept

moving as his friend opened a pair of heavy steel doors behind the autopsy table and began rummaging through the cupboards.

The girl was almost upon him. Richard put the book in his left hand and held it as high as he could. As she reached for it her body came into contact with his, pressing against him. Through his shirt Richard could feel the piercing ends of her splintered ribs digging into his skin. Every time she lunged for the book more shredded muscle rubbed off on him.

"Hurry up, Dev!" Richard choked. It was getting difficult to breath. Despite there being very little of her, the girl was strong and she was steadily crushing him in her attempts to get to the book. His nostrils stung with the odour emanating from her and he gagged as he tried to prevent himself from vomiting.

"Nearly there!" Dev's voice seemed an awfully long way away. "Can you push her away from you?"

"What do you think I've been trying to do?" Richard gasped.

"Then try harder!"

Still holding the book just out of reach, Richard squeezed his right hand in between himself and the gaping hollow of the girl's chest cavity. The heart and lungs were no longer there - he'd seen what remained of them fall from her.

It would have to be her spine, then.

Richard turned his hand palm outward and kept pushing it into the writhing body pressed against him until he came in contact with her vertebrae. They felt uncommonly rough, as if someone had been scratching at them with a carving knife.

Or gnawing.

No time to think about that at the moment, Richard told himself. He coughed and spluttered once more against the weight and smell of the twisting thing as he took in a breath to shout.

"Ready!"

"Okay." Dev's voice was muffled by the noises coming from the girl and Richard could only just hear him. "After three!"

Richard and waited for his friend to count. Then he summoned all his strength and shoved as hard as he could.

The corpse shot back and hit the mortuary slab with such force that it was bent backward over it. There was a crack as the thing's spine broke and its torso slipped to one side.

Unperturbed, it was about to make for Richard again when Dev smashed a gallon-sized bottle over its head and jumped out of the way.

"Cover your face!"

Richard did as he was told. Smokey yellow fumes were already beginning to envelop the creature. It raised bloody fingers to what was left of its skull, now a mess of brains, bone splinters and fragments of the brown glass bottle that Dev had hit it with.

"What is that stuff?" Richard coughed again, but this time it was due to the acrid fumes catching the back of his throat.

The creature tottered for a moment and reached out a hand to Richard, or rather the book, once more.

Then it fell to the floor.

Dev was on it immediately, covering it with the sheet that until a few minutes ago had been using to cover the part of the autopsy specimen he had not been working on.

The autopsy specimen that was now in pieces underneath him.

"Keep an eye on it." Dev moved to the back of the room and turned up the air conditioning. Soon the laminar flow had cleared the toxic fumes and the two men could breathe comfortably again.

"What was that?" Richard eyed the remains of the broken bottle sitting on the dissecting slab.

Dev shrugged. "No idea. But everything else in there is the size of a matchbox. I figured I could at least knock it out with a great big bottle."

"Knock it out? That was your great plan?"

Dev pointed at the crumpled mass at their feet. "It worked, didn't it? Mind you, the stuff in it obviously helped as well."

"Obviously." Richard realised he was still holding the book in his hand. "What do you think she wanted with this?"

Dev shook his head. "The question I think you meant to ask there was how did a girl who has been certifiably dead for over twelve hours and half dissected by my own good self come back to life?"

"Because of this - it has to be." Richard opened the book, then looked behind him.

"What are you doing now?"

"The last time I opened this book something very strange happened - I told you."

Dev looked over Richard's shoulder. "Well there's nothing there now."

Richard relaxed. "Perhaps it only happens in that room." He flicked through the pages. "I can't understand any of this."

"Looks like ancient Sumerian," Dev said, "with perhaps a smattering of the more obscure Aztec dialects."

Richard looked at him wide-eyed. "Really?"

Dev shook his head. "No of course not, you dingbat. Why would I know about shit like that?"

Richard couldn't help but laugh at that. Soon the two of them were in hysterics as the horrors of the last thirty minutes gave way to the relief that their lives were no longer in immediate danger.

But not for long.

"Do you agree it was the book that brought her back to life?" Richard said once they had calmed down.

"It's an insane explanation," Dev replied, "but this is turning into a pretty insane evening."

"I only ask because something's just occurred to me." Richard looked around him.

"And what's that?"

"How many more bodies have you got stored here at the moment?"

Dev's face fell as realisation struck.

"Oh, bollocks."

CHAPTER SEVEN

"There's nothing up here."

"What about lifting the ceiling tile?"

Dev gave the polystyrene board directly above his head a shove. It refused to budge.

"There isn't the space to fit a man's body in between these floors," he said. He tried a couple of other tiles that were close by with equal lack of success. "I agree those bumps in the floor looked like fingernails, but they must be something else."

They were in the side room below the one in which Arthur Lipscomb had disappeared. Richard was steadying a chair while his friend, who had insisted on inspecting the ceiling for any evidence that the man really had been dragged through the floor, checked the crawlspace.

"Why don't we check them for keratin?" Richard asked.

Dev looked down and shook his head. "Do you think I'm mad?" he said. "I'm not going back to that laboratory before the sun comes up, and only then with thirty policemen with me."

They had checked the storage lockers and, after finding no evidence of life amongst the frozen specimens currently in residence, both men had left the laboratory to investigate Mr Lipscomb's disappearance further. Richard had suggested calling the hospital's medical director and other officials but Dev had said no.

"All they're going to see is a patient you've lost and a body I've tried to dissolve in acid," was his quite sensible reasoning. "By the time we've completed all the paperwork that is going to generate, the world will have ended."

He had a point. And so here they were, having already inspected Mr Lipscomb's former room. As Richard had predicted, the symbols that the patient had drawn in blood had already been scrubbed away by nurses keen to get everything back to normal as soon as possible. All that remained were those curious bumps in the corner.

"Have you brought my nebuliser?" wheezed the old lady in the bed behind them.

"We'll get the nurse to fetch it for you in a minute," Richard said with the warmest smile he could muster.

"There's nothing here," said Dev, jumping down from the chair. "I don't know where we go now."

"Are you here to fix the plumbing, then?" came the breathless voice from behind them.

"No," said Richard. "We're just checking the ceiling for something."

"Horrible rattling old rubbish," the old lady continued. "I've been here for six weeks and it's never been as bad as tonight. I thought you were going to fix it. It's difficult enough for me to get a night's sleep as it is, what with my bad leg and my asthma. I've had asthma ever since I was little, you know."

"It doesn't seem to have hurt your ability to talk, though, has it?" said Dev.

"Jesus Christ." Richard hissed as he rolled his eyes. "No wonder you're a bloody pathologist."

"Why?" Dev asked as he was shunted out of the room. "What did I say?"

"Never mind." Richard shook his head and told the nurse on duty that Alberta Waterson needed her nebuliser.

"Oh don't worry," the young man replied. "She's just had one. Doesn't stop her going on about it, though."

Richard ignored Dev's raised eyebrows as they escaped the ward.

*

"Like I said, I don't know where we go from here."

"Well the first thing I need to do," said Richard, picking up the receiver of the corridor telephone, "is tell Sandra Harris I've lost her patient."

"Good luck with that one," said Dev as Richard punched in the number for the emergency operating theatres. "I'll be keeping a safe distance so her admonishing of you doesn't tear my ears off too."

It was Sandra who answered, but what she said was completely unexpected.

"Thank God! We need help up here now!"

"Sandra?"

There was a stunned pause, immediately followed by a sharp intake of breath. "That's not security, is it?"

"No," said Richard, shaking his head even though she couldn't see him. "It's Richard Dearden from A&E. What did you need security for?"

Somewhere in the distance he heard a crash and a scream.

"Because all bloody hell's broken loose up here, that's why!" came the reply.

Richard gripped the receiver so tightly he could feel the plastic threatening to crack. "What's happening up there?"

He could just make out what Sandra was saying over the noise. "It's insane. I can't even begin to tell you. Just find security and get them up here, would you? I don't know what else to do!"

There were more crashes and more screaming, this time

66

accompanied by a tearing sound. Richard could hear something large and heavy and wet moving around.

Then the line went dead.

"I really don't want to go up there," said Dev.

Richard was already running to the nearest lift. "How did you know I was going to suggest it?" he said.

His friend was struggling to keep up. "Oh, just by your general demeanour, and your tendency to want to go leaping in when unexplained, horrific, supernatural and above all seriously dangerous trouble rears its head. "

Richard thumbed the button. "I was actually going to suggest we go to the security lodge and find out what's happened to them but you're right - we might be able to help with whatever's going on up in the operating theatres."

Dev cursed as the lift doors slid open and they hurried inside.

They were so distracted they didn't see the crumpled body in the security uniform until the doors had closed and the lift was moving.

"Oh shit." Richard kept his distance but Dev was already slipping on a pair of latex gloves he had retrieved from his pocket.

"Something's caved his head in," he said as he examined the slumped form in the corner. "Heavy blow to the right parietal bone, causing a depressed skull fracture. Death would have been pretty quick. I've no idea what those giant sucker marks are from, though."

"Sucker marks?"

Dev pushed the body forward so Richard could see. Sure enough, around the neck and what was left of the face were several well-circumscribed welts the size of saucers.

"Do you think there's a giant octopus upstairs?"

Dev shook his head. "Probably best not to joke about that sort of thing, don't you think?"

The two men remained silent until the elevator doors slid open.

The white corridor in which they found themselves was brightly lit. A bloody smear along the wall ended at the body of another security guard. He was lying face down, with what remained of his right hand stretched in the direction of the elevators.

"Do you think any of them actually made it to where Sandra and the others are?" Richard asked as they stepped out.

"I think they all did," said Dev. "From the direction of the stains and the way in which he's lying I'd say these are the only two who made it back." He looked down to the end of the corridor, at the double doors marked 'Operating Theatres'.

Blood had seeped between them and was pooling on the floor.

"You still want to go down there?"

Richard nodded. "We both heard Sandra's voice. There could be more of them in there, still alive but trapped."

"Trapped by what is the question." Dev was examining the body of the corridor security man. "If I didn't know better I'd say something had taken a bite out of him."

"What sort of 'something'?"

Dev picked up what remained of the man's right arm, wincing as it came away at the shoulder. He held it up so Richard could take a better look and pointed at the deepest wound. "Something bit into his right arm here, taking the biceps and brachialis right down to the bone. You can see the humeral head where some of the shoulder attachments have gone, too."

Richard winced. He hadn't seen this much anatomical dissection since medical school. "...and to do this, the attacker would need teeth the size of?"

"A Bengal tiger," said Dev, looking over the rest of the limb before gently placing it back beside its owner. "Or something else with even more teeth."

"An octopus and a tiger," said Richard, wondering if coming here might just be the stupidest thing he had ever decided to do. "Perhaps someone's smuggled a zoo in here."

"Or a circus," said Dev. "Perhaps the emergency staff got bored and—"

There was a crash from somewhere in the distance. It was violent enough to make the theatre doors rattle.

Dev shivered. "Which one's being used for emergencies tonight?"

"Theatre fifteen." Richard was taking his pass card from his pocket. "I think it's a fair way in there."

"Sounds like it," said Dev. There was another crash, accompanied by a scream. "Remind me why we're here again?"

"Because we might be able to save some lives." Richard pressed his card against the flashing red security pad by the doors and waited until it turned green. "After you," he said.

"Oh, thanks." The ribbon of blood clot that filled the space between the two doors stretched and then broke into spatters as Dev pushed them apart.

Before them lay a scene of carnage.

"Do you know any of these people?" Dev didn't look up as he asked the question. He was too busy avoiding stepping on the torn and broken bodies scattered across the grey tiling.

Richard shook his head. "I don't spend much time up here," he said, "but it looks as if whatever's down there has got most of the emergency theatre staff."

As they made their way down the corridor, counting off operating theatres as they went, the mass of bodies began to thin out. However, the amount of blood sprayed on the walls and pooled on the floor increased.

"Looks like the lucky ones got as far as the door," said Richard.

"I have a feeling the lucky ones died first," said Dev as they reached a crossroads. They didn't need to look at the signs to see in which direction theatre fifteen lay. A trail of blood splashes, severed limbs and torn clothing told them they needed to turn to the right. Even if there hadn't been those gory signposts, it was also the direction the weird noise was coming from.

The combination of a rhythmic, heavy pounding, a whip crack, and a sucking noise was sufficient to make them both want to turn back.

"Do you think that's the octopus or the Bengal tiger?" Richard asked.

"Perhaps it's both," said Dev. "Perhaps one's eating the other."

There was a very human scream from just up ahead.

"Well, it was a nice idea while it lasted," said Richard.

The doors to theatre fifteen burst open and a man came running towards them, his hands clutched to his face, blood pouring from where his eyes had been. He pushed past them and ran down the corridor, bumping into the walls as he went and smearing himself with the blood of his slaughtered colleagues. He tripped over one of the prone bodies, fell to the floor, and was still.

Dev turned his attention back to the swinging door of theatre fifteen. He had to shout to be heard over the noises that were coming from inside. "Do we really want to go in there?"

"It's not a question of 'want', is it?" Richard edged towards the door and pushed it open.

In the far right hand corner, behind a trolley crammed with surgical instruments, crouched Sandra Harris. Her jet black hair was in disarray and her eyes were wild with anger. Beside her, cowering, Richard recognised Simon the house officer, three months out of medical school and more unprepared for what was happening now than anything else he had encountered since starting work at Northcote Park.

In the middle of the room lay an operating table that had been tipped on its side. He couldn't see the face of the surgical subject that was pinned beneath it, but the open hip wound was as empty of blood as the rest of the unfortunate patient's body probably was.

There was no-one else on the room.

But there was something.

It was over to the left, and Richard had to lean in further to try and make out exactly what it was.

A nest of tentacles, each as thick as a man's arm and able to reach right across the room, had taken root in the angle where the wall met the floor.

No, Richard thought, taken root wasn't right. They were emerging from the floor, as if they were part of a far greater creature that was concealed either behind this room or below it.

Or both.

Sandra spotted them at the door.

"Keep quiet!" she hissed.

As soon as she spoke the tentacles whipped towards her, the snaking coils probing at the flimsy trolley that was the only barrier between the creature and the two people behind it. Sandra grabbed a scalpel from one of the drawers and threw it at the nearest tentacle. It landed in the green-grey flesh with a dull thunk, causing the thing to recoil. She picked up another in readiness.

"They respond to sound vibrations!" she said as she prepared for another attack. "If you can find something to distract it we might have a chance!"

Dev picked up the closest thing to him, which happened to be a severed human arm, and flung it at the creature.

It sensed the flesh coming and raised the underside of two heavy tentacles in readiness. Dev had a view of suckers lined with sharp teeth as the limb was grabbed, torn apart, and wolfed down by those suckers-cum-mouths that were closest to the dripping flesh. Almost immediately the vast bulk quivered and two more tentacles sprouted forth.

"You idiot!" Sandra threw a device that looked a lot like a can-opener. "That's what it wants! You've made it grow even bigger!"

"Sorry!" Dev cried.

The tentacles snapped in his direction.

"Let's try this!" Richard grabbed a fire extinguisher from near the door and blasted the tendrils with a jet of very noisy carbon dioxide. The creature lashed at him and immediately recoiled as its flesh met with the jet of freezing gas.

"Good man!" Sandra yelled from the corner. "Keep it up and we'll try and get over to you!"

But the extinguisher had been designed to deal with nothing larger than a burning toaster or a smouldering waste paper basket. Three more squirts and it was empty.

With Sandra and Simon only halfway across the room.

"Oh God." It was the only thing Simon had said and it heralded him becoming frozen to the spot.

The tentacles swung round.

Sandra pulled at his arm. "Come on, Simon!"

The tentacles coiled back, preparing to tear both of them apart.

"Here, try this!" Dev had been outside and now he was back. He handed a new fire extinguisher to Richard and began blasting the creature with the other one he had found. The tentacles held their position as Sandra dragged Simon to safety.

"Thank god for fire safety training," she said once they were outside the operating theatre.

"Yes." Dev dropped the empty canister and rubbed his freezing hand. "I never thought I'd find myself saying that."

"Well thanks for thinking of it," Sandra said. "From both of us."

Richard gestured to the closed theatre doors. "What is that thing?"

Sandra gave him a look that said 'How the hell should I know?' before taking a deep breath and composing herself.

"It must have come out of the wall," she said. "It was only small at first. In fact nobody noticed it until one of the nurses backed into it and it bit her ankle. As soon as the thing latched on to her it grew. I knew it was a bad idea for her to try and pull it from the wall, but I was busy with the patient. As soon as she laid her hands on it the thing tore them from her wrists."

Richard nodded and didn't press her for any more. It

was easy to work out what had happened.

There was a thump on the door behind them.

"Sounds like our friend's waking up again." Dev peered through the window. "We should probably barricade this to stop it from getting out."

To the left was a steel cabinet used to house larger pieces of equipment. It was eight feet tall and it did the job nicely.

"That should do," said Sandra, "provided, of course that thing wants to come through the door."

"You mean it might eat through the wall?" Dev couldn't help sounding fascinated.

"That's how it got in. I'd imagine now that it's bigger it should be easier for it to push through the plaster."

"But where did it come from?" Richard was running his hands through his hair.

"I would have thought you'd be the last person asking that," said Dev. "You who's witnessed more weird shit this evening that anyone."

Sandra's gaze flicked to Richard. "What else have you seen?"

"Not just seen," said Dev. "We've had a bit of a close encounter ourselves."

Sandra concentrated as they told their tale of what had happened in the pathology lab. "So," she asked when they had finished, "do you still have this book you found?"

Richard pulled it from his pocket. "I thought it would be safest to keep it on me," he said.

Sandra took it from him and began leafing through it.

"Be careful!" Richard was already looking around him.

"What's the problem?"

"Apparently Richard had a little visitation when he opened the book in a side room downstairs," said Dev. "I didn't believe him then, but now I'd say it's quite possible."

"Thanks for that mate," said Richard, landing a thump on Dev's arm. "For the not believing me until you saw a walking corpse and a completely mental octopus to prove I could be telling the truth."

"Hey you were right about the octopus," said Dev, "How could I not believe you after that?"

"Well I don't feel anything behind me," said Sandra, looking up to see the two of them exchanging glances. "Oh for God's sake grow up, you two."

"Sorry Sandra." Dev peered over her shoulder. "If it makes you feel any better I can't see anything, either."

"It must have come from that side room," said Richard. "I can't help thinking that's where all this must have started."

"Well I can't understand a word of this." Sandra snapped the book shut and handed it back to Richard. "Load of old nonsense written in ink and blood and God knows what else."

"Blood?"

Sandra gave Dev a funny look. "Certainly looks like it. I would have thought you'd have spotted that."

Dev shook his head. "I didn't pay the book that much attention to be honest."

"Well it looks like blood to me," she continued. "Old blood on old parchment. That book could be hundreds of years old, or it could be something rigged up in the last week and soaked in cold tea to make it look that way. Bloody forgers will do anything to try and make a bit of easy money."

"I don't think this is a forgery," said Richard, tucking it away.

"Neither do I," said Sandra. "I do, however, think it's time to call the police."

Somehow Richard wasn't surprised when her mobile didn't work, or when they discovered that no-one else was capable of getting a signal.

"It's probably this place." Sandra looked around her. "It's always impossible to get a bloody signal here at the best of times, probably because of the girders they use to build these places. Let's try out on the fire escape."

"Is that right?" Dev whispered to Richard as the made their way back to the lifts and then on to where the corridor that ran the periphery of the floor led to the fire escape.

Richard shrugged. "Best not to question, though," he said, to which Dev nodded.

When they got to the peripheral corridor it quickly became obvious why no-one could get a signal.

The outside world had vanished.

CHAPTER EIGHT

"Maybe there's been a power cut." Dev was squinting through the glass, his breath steaming against the chill of the pane.

"If there has it's managed to knock out the moon and the stars as well." Sandra was shaking her head. "It's like someone's coated the whole building in black paint."

"Maybe that's what's happened." Richard was trying to think. He looked up and saw the disbelieving expressions of his two colleagues. "I don't mean literally," he said. "I mean something has succeeded in cutting this hospital off from the rest of the world."

Dev frowned. "What for?"

There was a groan from behind them, a mere semblance of words mumbled through lips too tired, or too scared, to work properly.

They turned to see Simon on his knees, clawing gently at the opposite wall.

"Bloody hell, Simon." Sandra tried to pull him to his feet, but he resisted. She managed to turn his face so they could hear what he was saying, though. Three words, repeated over and over.

"He...Is...Coming."

"What?" Sandra had taken Simon by the shoulders and was obviously resisting the urge to shake him. "Who is coming? What do you mean?"

"He can't hear you, Sandra." Richard crouched beside her and flashed a pen torch in the house officer's eyes. "There's no reaction," he said, doing it again. "See? His pupils don't even constrict. He's no longer with us."

"Then where is he?" That was Dev.

"I don't know." Richard turned to his friend. "Just because I've seen a few more weird things than you doesn't mean I have any more of a clue about any of this than you do."

"You have that book," said Sandra.

"Which no-one can read, yes." Richard looked back at Simon, who was picking at a crack in the plaster and whispering something into it. "I think we should probably stop him doing that," he said.

Sandra tried to pull Simon away but it was no good.

"I think I might need some help here, chaps," she said.

Sandra and Dev tried to pull Simon away.

Then Sandra and Dev and Richard tried to pull Simon away.

When Simon eventually moved, part of the wall came with him.

No, not part of the wall.

Part of Simon.

In a way.

"What the hell is that?" Sandra was staring in horror at the stretched pink elongations of the index and middle fingers of Simon's right hand, turning them into pale tentacles of flesh that reached as far as the wall, and disappeared into it.

"Something in the wall has merged with his fingers." Dev reached down to pull at them but Richard slapped him away. "Don't touch them!" he said. "You might end up like him!"

"What am I supposed to do, then?" Dev looked helpless. "We can't just leave him like that."

"I think a surgical solution is needed here." Sandra took out a small pocket knife, opened one of the blades, and cut smartly through the things that were attaching Simon to the wall.

A scream akin to that of a pig being slaughtered filled the air. All three looked at Simon, but the desperate cry wasn't coming from him.

It was coming from the crack in the wall.

"Sounds as if something isn't very happy about that," said Sandra, putting the knife away.

As the other two helped Simon to his feet he began to mumble. "Not happy...not happy...no...no...no... nonononononononono."

"No-one's very happy at the moment, my friend." Dev tried to calm Simon down while wrapping a handkerchief around the stumps of his severed, spurting fingers. "Just keep still so I can stop the bleeding, would you?"

But Simon didn't want to keep still. With an inhuman effort he shrugged off both Dev and Richard, and ran back to the crack, reaching through with his bleeding fingers to clutch at whatever lay beyond it.

"Don't...leave...me!" Simon's cries were pitiful as he tried to push himself through the widening gap in the plaster.

"Don't just stand there you two!" Sandra's voice jerked the two men into action, but even as they stepped towards him, Simon began to disappear, not just through the crack.

He began to merge with the wall itself.

"What should we do now?" Dev was the first to reach Simon, or rather the semi-human thing that had now melded with the brickwork.

"Pull him back! Sandra cried.

It was like trying to pull the wall itself. Simon kept biting at them, and struggled with all his might as Richard and Dev hung onto his arms with grim desperation. Finally, the house officer emitted a bloodcurdling scream as his body slid away from them and was sucked into the depths of the building.

Leaving Dev and Richard holding the arm that had detached itself to allow the rest of Simon's body to be consumed by whatever was living in the concrete.

It took a moment for them to register what had happened. Then they dropped the limb. It fell to the ground with an unnaturally soft sound. When they looked again the arm was crumbling into a fine powder.

"Not a drop of blood left in it," Richard whispered, unable to take his eyes off the heap of grey dust that was already starting to disappear.

"Not a drop of anything by the look of it," said Dev. "No blood, no tissue fluid, nothing. It's been drained." He looked at the crack in the wall only to discover it had now vanished. "That's probably what's happened to the rest of him as well."

There was a rumble beneath them.

"We need to get out of here." Sandra was making her way back down the corridor.

"And go where, Sandra?" Richard was running after her. "The last time we checked the world outside has ceased to exist."

"I don't know!" Sandra was fighting back tears of frustration. "Just away from here, away from all that death in the operating theatre, away from that...that thing, and away from - " she bit her lip and fought back a sob, " - away from what happened to Simon."

"What happened to Simon could be happening all over this hospital." The thought had entered Richard's mind as soon as Simon had begun acting strangely but he hadn't had the courage to voice it until now. "If you try and get to the ground floor you might not make it, and even if you do there's nowhere to go from there."

"Well we can't just stand here and do nothing!" Sandra grabbed the book from his pocket, flicked through the pages once more, and then threw it to the ground. "Fucking thing!" She gave it a hateful look. "If only it was in English we might be stand a chance of stopping this."

"That's a good idea," said Dev.

They both turned to him.

"What is?" Richard asked.

"Turning it into English." Dev picked the book up. "We could scan it in and post it up on the internet, with a big flashing "Help Us" notice at the top. You never know - it's possible some expert in this stuff is burning the midnight oil and is as bored as most of us usually are at this time."

"Great idea, Dev." Richard didn't look convinced. "You've forgotten one thing. If there's no mobile phone signal chances are there's no broadband either, or landline."

"Besides," said Sandra. "If we could get a message out of here wouldn't it be a better idea just to contact the police?"

"How much help do you think the police are going to be against an other-dimensional being that's living in the fabric of this building and sucking people dry?" Dev probably sounded harsher than he intended.

"If that's even what's happening," said Richard. "But Dev's got a point, and we haven't actually tried a hospital computer yet."

"God help us," said Sandra. "They still run on Windows XP, you know."

Richard smiled. "Then perhaps it'll be old enough to help us combat whatever ancient force old Mr Lipscomb seems to have conjured up."

"Do we even know where there's one with a scanner attached?" Dev was already nodding as they made their way back down the corridor.

"In my office," he said. "Next door to the mortuary."

"Oh charming," Sandra replied. "From one repository of death to another."

"That's the spirit." Richard was calling the lift.

An uncomfortable silence descended as they waited for the flashing digital number to the left of the doors to reach their floor. When it did the doors failed to open.

"Bloody things." Dev punched the call button again. "Maybe they're jammed." He gave them a kick.

"Or maybe something's holding them shut," said Sandra, one second too late as the doors slid open and the fungoid remains of the security guard both Dev and Richard had forgotten was in there threatened to envelop them in a cloud of filthy spores. The fleshy horror that had grown into the corner of the lift raised an atrophied stump of an arm. Its fingers had been replaced with nests of friable hyphae the colour of poisoned earth that burst as the thing rocked from side to side.

Richard pushed Dev aside as the spores settled on the white floor tiles, turning their points of contact a sickly grey colour that began to spread towards them.

Dev was backing away. "I think we'd better try the stairs instead."

The staircase next to the elevators had no windows, and only a dim flickering light that looked as if it was about to give out to show them the way.

Sandra peered into the gloom and wrinkled her nose. "Perhaps we should try the stairs on the other side of the building?"

Richard didn't think so. "If we leave it any longer those spores will have made it here and we'll have lost this escape route."

That was the decision made, then.

"Is your office far?" Sandra took a step inside and shivered. It was cold in the stairwell, and there was a damp feel to the air that Richard knew was entirely wrong.

"Just the next floor down," Dev said, following Richard and bringing up the rear.

"I've always wondered why they put the operating theatres on the top floor." Sandra had only made it down three steps, and already she was having to avoid pools of moisture that had collected on the concrete.

"To keep you lot away from the rest of us of course," Dev replied.

Sandra wasn't going to let him get away with that. "They should have you and your dead bodies in the basement where you belong."

They were all doing their best to keep their spirits up, just as the worsening cold and damp and darkness was doing its best to fill them with terror. Sandra was about to start the second flight that would lead to the floor below when the darkness won.

"Bugger."

"Hang on," Richard said. A moment later the light from his pen torch showed her the way.

"Thanks." Six more steps and they were down. Sandra pushed gingerly at the fire door. It swung open noiselessly into the darkened floor beyond.

"How long will the batteries in that thing last?" Dev whispered to Richard.

"No idea. Let's just get to your office as quickly as possible, shall we?"

"In that case give me the torch so I can see where I'm going."

Richard handed it over, and Dev took that as his cue to take the lead. "It's just down here on the left," he said.

"It's bloody quiet," Sandra said, whispering because the other two were.

"It's a pathology department," said Dev, shining the torch ahead of them. "It's always like this."

The light cast flickering shadows, creating shapes suggestive of the monstrosities they had seen upstairs. Each time they came upon one, Richard had to throw something at it to convince the others of its insubstantiality before they could proceed, and it was another ten minutes before they found themselves facing a glass paned door with the words "Dr D Choudry - Consultant" stencilled on it.

"Have you got your keys?" Sandra hissed.

"Don't need them." Dev pushed the door open. "I never lock it."

The light switch didn't work.

"That's not very encouraging." Richard shone the pen torch around the room. The beam was noticeably dimmer than it had been out in the corridor. "We're going to need to find another one of these soon," he said.

The dim glow allowed Dev to find his desk, and to switch his desk lamp on.

"Different circuit, better access to the backup generators," he explained, "which should hopefully mean..."

He thumbed the startup button on the computer. The green light flashed on, then off. Then it came it again for five seconds, turned yellow, and went off again.

"It always does that." Dev glanced at the other two's worried faces. "Give it another minute."

Sure enough, the green light started to again, and now the screen began to show signs of activity as well. Soon Dev's desktop appeared, the icons bold little chinks of blue against a picture of a Dev himself in a sombrero.

"Very fetching," said Sandra without a trace of amusement.

"Important to keep the work environment a bright and happy place," said Dev as he typed in passwords, clicked on an icon, and opened his bottom right hand desk drawer.

Richard peered over Sandra's shoulder."Why do you keep your scanner in there?"

"Because if I didn't it would have gone walkies by now." Dev lifted the lid and held out his hand for the book. "How many pages should I scan?"

As the other two were both shrugging Richard had an idea. He took the book back and flicked through it until he came across something that resembled the pattern Arthur Lipscomb had drawn on the floor of the side room.

"Just put the picture up," he said. "And then maybe post it with 'Found a picture that looks like this - need help,' or something like that."

The machine hummed.

"Any thoughts as to where I'm supposed to be posting it?" Dev was clicking on his browser icon.

"Let's see if there's a connection first, shall we?" Sandra had crossed her fingers, and Richard was surprised to realise that he had as well. They stood behind Dev and waited.

And waited.

"It's thinking about it," said Dev.

"Are you sure?" Sandra pointed at the black screen."It looks as if it's crashed to me."

"You're going to tell us it always does that, aren't you?" said Richard.

Dev sighed. "Actually it never does that. Usually I get a notice from security telling me all the sites I shouldn't have visited using the hospital network the last time I was on here. A blank screen is not good news."

The computer made a few grinding noises and a tiny egg timer appeared.

"Well it's doing something," said Sandra. "Who knows - in a minute we might get to find out exactly why Dev likes wearing sombreros."

"Least of my worries at the moment." Dev tapped the table with a pen. Richard was about to ask him to stop when the screen flickered and a home page appeared.

"Thank God." Sandra let out a sigh of relief.

"And no message from security!" said Dev, beaming. "But then it has been a busy week."

"Have you got university access on here?"

Dev nodded. "What's on your mind, Richard?"

"Just that, rather than post on some message board or social networking site that's likely to get you more unhelpful comments than anything else, how about finding an appropriate university department and asking for help there?"

"Brilliant idea," Dev nodded. "Except which department should we try?"

"All of them," said Sandra. "We're desperate."

Richard shook his head. "If we carpet bomb the university network the spam filters will just dump it and then we'll have no hope of sending it again."

"How about this?" Dev had accessed the university's department list and was resting the mouse arrow on one.

"'Department of Ancient Languages'," Sandra read. "Go on, then, although I can't imagine there'll be anyone looking at their discussion forum at this time of night."

"You never know," said Dev. "Perhaps they're all there now."

"They're academics," said Sandra. "I bet you whoever might be able to help us is probably turning over in bed now after eight hours' sleep and looking forward to their next seven."

"Well it's on there now," said Dev. "I put a new discussion subject of HELP NEEDED URGENTLY. In capitals. Now all we have to do is wait."

There was a rumbling noise from somewhere beneath them.

"How long should we give them?" Sandra asked.

Richard looked at his watch, and then wondered why. "We give them until we have any better idea of what to do," he said. "I don't think any of us are going anywhere anytime soon."

The rumbling came again. This time a little louder. Was it Richard's imagination or did the building shake a little this time?

"We've got a message!"

Sandra and Richard crowded round the monitor as Dev clicked on the reply. As they read it, their collective expressions formed a collage of confusion.

- U Suck Balls

If there was any doubt as to the sender's intentions, this was wiped away by the second message, which followed rapidly after the first.

- No ReAlly, U hav Major Suckage of big Harry Balls

"That's what you get for your discussion board not having a password, I guess." Dev pinched the bridge of his nose. "We could try somewhere else?"

Richard shrugged. "Sure," he said. There was nothing else to do.

Dev tried to move off the page but a flashing cursor signified another message being typed in. The browser was so slow they had to wait for it to finish before they could exit.

- Suky sucky ballsy walls u can suk my—-I'm terribly sorry for that. If you're still there please DON'T HANG UP or whatever passes for that on these computer things. I have my grandson staying with me and he is the one responsible for the quite obscene messages you have been receiving. I can offer you my apologies later, but right now I need to verify something with you. Is your request for help serious? Is that combination of sigils exactly what you found? Please be honest as you could potentially be in a very serious situation.

"There is a God," breathed Sandra.

"Not necessarily," said Dev, tapping away. "It could just be the same person having more of a laugh. Let's try this."

- Can verify we are in serious trouble. Pattern found on floor drawn in blood. Not sure if exactly the same but similar. Now in dire situation. Who are you & can you prove it?

It took what felt like an age for the next message to come through.

- Brian Degville, Prof. of Cabbalistic & Esoteric Studies. My PhD was entitled Sumerian Sigils: A Retranslation in Light of Further Evidence. It got me my post here. What you have there isn't Sumerian, though. It's something far older and far more obscure. In fact I would be hard pressed to say which part of the world it originated from, partly because we believe the world was a very different place when it was suggested to have be written.

Sandra opened her mouth to say something but Dev was already typing again.

- We are in Northcote Hospital. Cut off from outside world. Ritual shown above seems to have triggered something. Monsters roam the hallways and are killing us. Situation is desperate. What can we do?

It took even longer for the reply to come through this time. But the message they received was the shortest of the lot.

- Nothing.

CHAPTER NINE

Another rumble echoed through the building, definitely vibrating the structure this time and causing Richard's innards to convulse.

No, he thought, it wasn't the building moving that had caused that. It was what was on the screen.

"What does he mean, nothing?" Sandra looked so incensed it was almost funny, until Richard realised he was probably on the border of hysteria.

"Let's ask him, shall we?" said Dev. "After all, if we're doomed, we've got nothing better to do."

This time they had to wait even longer, which was either a good sign, meaning that Professor Degville was typing a lot, or bad, because it meant he had gone to bed. Finally, after numerous attempts at refreshing the page, there was a new message from him.

- It's difficult to say anything with certainty as regards these ancient documents, but the consensus is that the further back one goes, the simpler these rituals become. Therefore, in order to stop such a process from moving forward, one has to move it backward. This would have to be achieved by the drawing of the symbols in reverse, by which I mean an exact mirror image of what was originally created. However, I fear this may be impossible. Even if you were able to remember the exact pattern of symbols that were reproduced on your hospital side room floor, the reversal of the ritual would require that it include some of the blood that fashioned it. (By the way, I would give my left arm for a chance to read the book you have in your possession, though I suspect, that will not be possible anytime soon).

"No it won't," said Dev. "Seeing as the two things we need have disappeared, one wiped away by an overzealous nurse and the other absorbed into the floorboards according to you."

Richard gave him a gloomy nod. "If I'd known this was going to happen I'd have drawn it before she—-" He took out his mobile as realisation struck. "I took a picture of it!" He scrolled through until he came to it and held is up so the others could see.

"It's a bit blurry at the edges." Dev was squinting at it. "But it's better than nothing."

"Too bloody right it is." Sandra nudged Dev's shoulder. "Tell him we've got a picture of it."

- We've got a picture of it. On a mobile phone.

- Excellent! But you still need the blood of the one who drew it.

- Bugger. We'll get back to you.

"Is there no way of getting some of this bloke's blood?" Sandra looked from Dev to Richard.

Richard shook his head. "He's gone," he said. "Dev and I looked. There's not a trace of him apart from a few fingernails."

"Will fingernails work?"

Dev typed it in.

- No. Sorry.

"Didn't Simon give him a blood transfusion?" Sandra was trying to think.

"Yes," said Richard. "That's what he used, at least in part, to draw the thing in the first place."

"So he must have had a blood sample taken for cross-matching?" she looked at Dev, for whom the penny had also dropped.

"Of course he would have! And," he looked at Richard, "you ordered a whole load of other blood tests on him as well, didn't you?"

Now Richard was nodding as well. "And any blood samples that are taken—"

"Get stored for forty-eight hours!" they all said together.

Dev started typing.

- We can get a tiny amount of his blood. Would that be enough?

- I have no idea. This kind of thing hasn't exactly been performed very often, and the texts are vague on the matter owing to them being so ancient most of what was written has faded to nothing. But it is certainly worth trying. The sigils still need to be drawn in blood, however, so you will need to mix his in with somebody else's.

"There's plenty of blood around here at the moment," said Sandra. "We just have to scoop some off the walls."

"Best not." Richard wasn't sure if she was joking. "We've seen how those spores spread. Chances are anyone who's been killed by these things will probably have become infected by them."

Sandra shook her head. "What the hell is actually threatening us anyway?"

They turned back to the computer and Dev typed in her question.

- That's more difficult to say, and even more fascinating. The translated texts make reference to another reality, or plane of existence if you like, filled with things that are the very opposite of what we have in this world. These things are filled with a terrible rage, a terrible jealousy that causes them to constantly pick and dig at the delicate membrane that separates the two universes. But they can never cross, unless, of course, they have help. From this side.

"So basically it's all a bit Lovecraft," said Dev.

"Who?" said the other two together.

"Never mind," said Dev.

"So to summarise," said Richard. "We need Arthur Lispcomb's blood samples from the fridge in the lab, a couple of bags of blood from the blood bank, and a huge amount of luck."

"Sounds about right to me," said Sandra.

"Looks that way," said Dev

- Good luck. (said Professor Degville on the screen).

"One last thing," said Richard. "Could you ask the professor if we need to draw this thing anywhere in particular?"

Dev typed it in. The reply came as no surprise.

- I have absolutely no idea.

"Well, we'll worry about that once we've got the blood." Sandra looked at Dev. "What a stroke of luck - I'm guessing it's stored up here somewhere?"

Dev nodded. Then he saw Richard shaking his head, realised his mistake, and copied his friend.

"Where is it, then?"

"There was no more room in the fridge up here," said Richard. "So I took it back down to the emergency department where they could look after it in their fridge for the night."

Sandra glared at Richard in disbelief. "The emergency department?"

"Yes."

"The one that's on the ground floor?"

"Yes."

"While we're stuck up here on the fifth?"

"We could take the lift?" Dev suggested.

"You mean the one with our friend the fungus creature in it? Or perhaps we could try a different one that might have something else horrible hiding behind the doors?"

95

There was a pop and the image on the screen faded to a dot before vanishing.

"Or," Sandra continued, "perhaps we should forget that idea altogether because now it looks as if all the power to this building is failing, which means we could be stuck between floors and running out of air, while some bloody tentacled thing tries to get at us."

"Okay, Sandra, you've made your point." Richard did his best to keep his voice calm. He obviously wasn't the only one close to losing it. They waited a moment for the auxiliary power to kick in. It took what felt like an eternity for the room to become bathed in a dull red glow that came from the corridor.

"That'll be the secondary backup for this floor, but it looks as if it's nearly at zero," said Dev. "Oh, and what was Sandra's point exactly?"

Richard rolled his eyes at Dev. "We're going to have to take the stairs," he said.

There was a crash from outside, then something began hammering on the door.

Something that left a smear of dirty-looking blood on the glass with each blow.

"Sounds like the rest of my customers have woken up," said Dev, without a trace of mirth.

As if to prove him right, more shapes appeared outside the door - scratching and tapping.

"That glass isn't going to last long." Sandra was rooting through the desk drawers. "Do you keep anything in here we could use as a weapon?"

Dev pulled out his desk drawer completely and emptied the contents on the floor. Then he handed her the drawer itself. "How about whacking them with one of these?"

Sandra took it from him. "Better than nothing," she said.

"I don't suppose either of you smoke?" An idea had just occurred to Richard, only for it to be dashed by his colleagues shaking their heads. "In that case Dev, I don't suppose you keep a box of matches in here anyway, do you?"

"No," said Dev, down on his knees and searching through the detritus of what he had just tipped on the floor. "But I've got a cigarette lighter around here somewhere if that's any use."

Richard tried to ignore the sounds coming from the door. "It would be perfect," he replied.

"Why do you keep a lighter if you don't smoke?"

"To light my Bunsen burner, baby." Dev gave Sandra a hint of a tired smile as he tossed the red plastic cylinder he had found over to Richard. "Plus sometimes the automatic ignition thing fails on some of our incubators. They keep saying they'll fix it but until then..." his voice tailed off. "Richard, what are you doing?"

"Something that might buy us some breathing space out there." Richard had the book in his left hand and the lighter in his right. "After all, your post mortem specimen was very keen to get hold of this, wasn't she? Perhaps if we threaten them with its imminent destruction they'll back off."

He edged towards the door.

"I need someone to open it."

Neither Sandra nor Dev looked keen.

"Richard," Sandra didn't look convinced by his plan, "why don't you just burn the book anyway?"

"Because if we do there's a good chance we'll never get things back to the way they were. Now come and open the door so I don't have to spend any longer standing here terrified than I have to."

Sandra edged closer, with Dev right behind her.

97

"You sure you want to do this?"

Two blows hit the glass in rapid succession and a large crack appeared.

"No." Richard licked his lips. "But at the moment it's all we've got."

Sandra grasped the door handle. "I'm going to count to three," she said.

Richard nodded.

"One."

Another thump against the door from something fleshless and brittle caused the crack to lengthen.

"Two."

The next blow made the crack even bigger. Fragments of glass fell to the floor.

"Three."

Sandra gave the door a savage pull and the glass fell out completely. Richard held the book out in front of him and sparked the lighter. Yellow flame erupted from the plastic barrel and illuminated the area ahead of them for six feet. He was glad it didn't reveal much more than that.

Backing away from the flame that threatened to lick the pages of the book held oh-so-precariously close to it, was the most monstrous collection of individuals any of them had ever seen. Each bore the characteristic Y-shaped incision that showed they had undergone an autopsy, but otherwise they all differed greatly.

There were victims of road accidents, of other brutalising traumas, of wasting diseases, cancer, infection, and of any number of terminal conditions. They all backed away as Richard threatened the object they were obviously so desperate to get hold of.

"Seems to be working," said Sandra.

Richard could only offer a nod as he kept his eye on the creatures surrounding them, their dead flesh bathed in the yellow glow of the flame.

"Which way to the stairs, Dev?"

"Best to go back the way we came," hissed the reply. "There's another staircase around the other side of the building but it's further away."

"Okay. Everyone watch each other's backs."

Slowly, step by step, the three of them began to shuffle back down the corridor.

And the undead army shuffled with them, keeping a distance, but never more than a few feet away.

"Have we got much further to go?" His eyes on the book and the flame, Richard was having to rely on his friends to guide him backwards.

"Yes." Sandra never did have a good line in being reassuring.

"They're getting closer," said Dev. "For every step we take they're closing the gap. By the time we get to the stairs they'll be on top of us."

"In that case," said Sandra, "what are they going to do?

"I've got an idea," said Dev. "But I should warn you right now that it's really, really, dangerous."

"If the only alternative is death then let's go for it." Sandra laid a hand on Richard's shoulder. "You game, Richard?"

"I'll have to be," he replied, hoping it didn't involve another large jar of acid.

Slowly, with the undead gaining on them all the time, Dev guided them to the wall, and began to feel his way along to the right. Eventually, he found what he was looking for.

"In here," he said, turning the door handle and ushering them inside. He used a fire extinguisher to provide a temporary barricade and put his back against it as well.

Sandra looked around in the dim light. "Dev, this is just another room you've trapped us in."

"Is there another way out?" Richard put the lighter away, grateful to give his heated fingertips a rest.

Dev shook his head. Behind him the door threatened to cave inwards. Sandra glared at him.

"Then what are we doing in here?"

"This is one of the specimen preparation rooms," he said. "It's where we do a lot of the section cutting and staining, but the reason we're in here is because of that big oven at the back."

The others turned to look at the shape looming in the distant dimness.

"The incubator," said Richard.

"That runs on gas," said Sandra.

Dev nodded. "Right. If we can get them all in here with the gas turned on, then maybe we've got a chance."

"Of blowing ourselves up you mean?"

"I think we can move faster than them," Dev said to Sandra. "I also think it's our only chance of getting off this floor."

Richard walked up to the oven and grasped the heavy stainless steel handle. The door swung open with a creak.

"There's a tap on the back to turn the gas on." Dev was now visibly straining to keep the door closed. "Whatever you do, don't use the lighter to find it."

Richard shook his head and felt round for the feed pipe. Once he had found it, he ran his fingertips along until he came to the tap.

"Turn it until it's completely parallel with the pipe."

A hiss began to come from the oven.

"How long should we wait?" Sandra was already covering her nose.

"I think this door is going to dictate that more than we are," said Dev. "Richard, you're going to need to be the bait again, I'm afraid."

"You mean the book is," Richard corrected.

"Of course, but seeing as you've got it and you're nearest the oven..."

"Don't mention it," Richard said. "Perhaps the two of you would care to herd them my way?"

They didn't need to. With the pressure finally too much, Dev was thrown forwards as the fire extinguisher fell to the floor and the autopsy specimens shambled in.

They headed straight for Richard.

"Toss the lighter over here!" Dev was holding his hands out, close to the door, as the dead ignored him.

"You'll never see to catch it!" Richard had the book held out at arm's length as he moved to the left of the hissing incubator. He coughed as the odour of methane caught in the back of his throat.

"Oh for goodness' sake let me." Sandra pushed through the corpses, took the lighter, and made her way back to Dev.

"Right," Dev was edging out of the room. "When I say now, throw the book to me."

Richard cringed. The creatures were almost upon him

"Only if you say it very soon!" he said in between coughs. "I can hardly bloody breathe!"

"Should be enough, then," Dev shouted over the mass of semi-dissected bodies. "Nice expert throw for me, now!"

Richard could barely see Dev, let alone where his hands might be. He held the book as high as he could, flicked his wrist back, and threw it as hard as he could.

The book sailed through the door, over Dev and Sandra's heads, and out into the corridor.

"Run!"

Richard didn't need Dev to tell him. He took a deep breath and shoved between the monsters filling the room, trying to ignore the bony fingers plucking at his clothing, almost as if the book had left some trace of its passing on him.

"Come on!" Dev had the lighter in one hand. In the other he had his wallet, from which a twenty pound note was protruding.

"What the hell are you going to do?" Sandra looked at him in horror as Richard came pelting through the doorway. He picked the fire extinguisher up and hurled it at the front line of walking corpses. They fell back into the room.

"That should hold them for all of ten seconds," he said as they retreated down the corridor.

"Can you smell gas?" Dev asked.

"Not as bad as in that room," Sandra replied.

"Let's hope it's not bad enough." Dev flicked the little ridged wheel and the lighter sparked into life. Much to everyone's obvious relief they weren't enveloped in a blinding explosion.

"Now," Dev said, lighting the money. "Let's hope that

there is enough down there to stop our friends for good."

The flame flared up, giving them more light.

It also revealed the creatures crawling over one another in their desperate attempts to get out of the room.

"I never realised money burned so easily," said Dev as he threw the wallet overarm into the melee. Then he dived to the floor to join the others.

The explosion rocked the building, made plaster fall from the ceiling, and caused the three of them to be enveloped in a mixture of smoke, dust and blasted body parts.

When the smoke had cleared enough for them to see, they got to their feet.

"Well that showed them," said Dev, brushing himself down.

"You really think so?"

Richard and Dev followed Sandra's gaze to the rubble further down the corridor.

There were moving body parts trying to escape from it.

Moving body parts that were being manipulated by tentacles that emerged from the cracks in the walls and ceiling.

"Let's get to the stairs," said Richard, but the others were already on their way. Sandra made it into the stairwell first, and gave a triumphant cry as she peered down the steps.

"Hey! I think there's still lighting on the next floor down!"

They took the steps two at a time, eager to get away from what they had just witnessed and the cloying darkness it inhabited.

"You never know," said Dev as they pushed open the door to get onto the third floor. "Maybe only the top two floors have been affected so far. Perhaps the third floor's still safe."

But it wasn't.

CHAPTER TEN

The lights were still on, and that was a good thing.

The rest was all bad.

The friable fungus that had consumed the security guard in the lift was much more widespread here. Rubbery growths of an unhealthy greenish-grey clung to the walls and hung in precarious stalactite formations from the ceiling. In many places it had grown to cover the fluorescent light fittings. The electricity was still fighting its way through, but it had the effect of rendering the corridor they were standing in the colour of the grave. It was obviously acting as an insulator as well, as it was noticeably warmer down here.

"Shouldn't be surprised I suppose," said Sandra, wiping her brow. "This is the floor we had Arthur Lipscomb admitted to."

"Yes," said Richard. "But his room is way over on the other side of the hospital."

"Which means the rest of this floor is probably worse than this." Dev's voice was grim. "We should probably keep going down."

"What about the people on the wards?"

Dev shook his head. "If it's like this here, miles away from Arthur Lipscomb's room, that stuff is probably running riot over every ward between here and there. If we try and help them we'll just end up consumed by it ourselves."

Sandra gave him a cold look. "That's a bit harsh," she said.

John Llewellyn Probert

"Okay," Dev was stepping down the corridor, taking care to avoid the bigger lumps of fibrous matter. He stopped and pointed at a carpet of dripping fungoid tissue that coated the wall. "I can just make out the sign that says 'Respiratory Ward 3'. Do you honestly think there's anyone in there who's still breathing? I can't even see the doors!"

"That still makes you a harsh bastard," Sandra hissed. "You don't have to be quite so callous."

"Listen to who's talking!" Dev might as well have had a red rag waved in front of him. "The only orthopaedic registrar ever to get told off for being insensitive by Professor 'Bastard' McCleod, a man who didn't even go to his own mother's funeral because, to quote the great man himself, 'the bloody woman didn't deserve it'!"

"Will you two stop that!" Richard tried to ignore the headache that was building up behind his frontal bone. "We should get down to the ground floor and do what Professor Degville told us." He winced as he turned back to the stairs, a sudden pain in his right hip causing him to draw breath.

"Sorry, Richard," Dev called out, before lowering his voice to Sandra. "And I'm really sorry about that. I think all of this is starting to get to me a bit."

"A bit?" Sandra's expression softened. "It should be getting to you a lot. I know it is to me. Looks like it's affecting Richard as well."

"It is," Richard groaned from the door to the stairs. "But that's not what's hurting right at this moment." He leaned against the doorway, the pain in his hip worsening by the second.

"Are you all right?" Dev was just behind Sandra.

"Have you broken something?" she asked.

"I don't think so." Richard winced as she pressed his right thigh.

106

"Does it hurt there?"

"Not as much as it does higher up."

Sandra moved her hand upwards carefully until it came to rest over the book in the pocket of Richard's white coat.

When she touched it he nearly screamed.

"You need to get this coat off," she said.

"I'd like to," said Richard, "but somehow I don't think the book is going to let that happen."

"What do you mean?" Dev was looking concernedly at his friend.

"I think the book wants to stay on this floor, and the further I try to move away from it, the more pain it's going to give me."

"That's ridiculous."

Richard nodded. Sandra was right, but nevertheless he knew it was the truth.

"It's not going to be any crazier than anything else we've witnessed tonight," said Dev. "Do you mind if I try to take it out of your pocket?"

"Why not?" Richard shrugged. "And thanks for not suggesting I do it myself. Every time the damn thing moves it hurts like hell. It feels as if it's welded to my skin through the material." He held onto the door frame for support as Dev reached out with tentative fingers to try and pull the pocket away from his side.

It didn't want to come.

Richard gave a gasp that became a yell as Dev tried to pull the adherent material, and the book it contained, away from Richard's skin. Dev relaxed for a moment to give Richard a breather, then crouched down close beside him.

"I'm going to do that again," he said.

"Oh thanks," Richard replied. "I can't wait."

"But I'm going to do it much more gently, and at the same time I'm going to try and see what's causing it to stick to you."

Sandra handed Richard a pen. "Bite on that if it'll help," she said.

"All that will do is give me a mouthful of ink," Richard said with a gasp of laughter. "But why don't you try and pull the coat away while Dev gets down on his hands and knees and has a proper look?"

That sounded reasonable to all concerned, and so Richard braced himself once more, digging his fingertips into the staircase doorpost as Sandra tried to pull his coat away and Dev did his best to inspect the area.

"Can you see anything?" Richard spoke through gritted teeth.

"Amazing," was all Dev could say.

"What?"

"Your coat has got stuck to your trousers." Dev pushed the area apart gingerly. "Does that hurt?" A cry from Richard confirmed that it did. "There are tiny, flesh-like protrusions extending from your coat pocket and into the flesh of your thigh." Dev looked in Richard's pocket. When he looked up again his face was grim.

"It looks as if the book has become attached to you, quite literally."

Richard felt his stomach flip over. "You mean it's growing into me?"

"Looks like it." Dev shook his head. "Your guess is as good as mine as to what we do about it."

Sandra already had her pocket knife out. "I'll cut it away now if you like."

If Richard had felt ill before, now he really wanted to throw up. "Is it sharp?" he gulped.

Sandra showed him the shining blade, as if somehow that would help. "I keep it as sharp as any surgical instrument," she said. "In case of emergencies. Which this most definitely is."

"Hang on," Dev wasn't looking too happy. "Didn't you use that to cut whatever was dragging Simon into the wall?"

Sandra nodded. "Why?"

"Well, it might have traces of him on it. I thought you orthopods worried about infection control more than anyone else."

"They should certainly have some more sterile kit down in the emergency department." To Richard's infinite relief, Sandra folded the knife and put it away. "Are you going to be able to wait that long?"

Richard had no idea. "I'll be fine," he said. "And if you need to take my leg off down there I'm sure they have a bone saw." It was meant to be a joke, but the words felt dead even as they left his lips.

"Do you need a hand?"

Richard waved Dev's hand away as he experimented with putting his weight on the affected hip. "It doesn't seem quite as bad, now," he said. "But if I need help I'll let both of you know." He looked down the stairwell. "We should get going."

They set off, Richard behind Dev in case he fell, with Sandra bringing up the rear.

"I'm wondering what we'll find on the next floor down," Dev said as they took slow, measured steps, mainly because Richard couldn't go any faster, but partly because they were all trepidant about what the second floor might contain.

"More of the same, probably". Sandra had her hand deep in her pocket, presumably clutching the knife she was starting to rely on as an object of comfort.

"I'm not so sure." There was obviously something on Dev's mind. He came to a halt with another flight to go before they reached the next floor down. "We've had monsters on the fifth floor, right?" The others nodded. "And walking dead on the fourth."

"Moved about by those tentacles, though," Sandra pointed out.

"That was only after we blew a hole in the ceiling," Richard said. "We shouldn't forget that. What's your point, Dev?"

"Well, we've had weird fungus stuff on the third." Dev gave into the urge to rub his chin. "Have you ever read Dante's *Divine Comedy*?"

"We don't need to have read it to know what you're getting at," said Sandra.

Richard caught on. "You mean the whole nine circles of hell, thing?"

"Something like that," said Dev. "But obviously not on the same scale."

"You never know," Sandra said, "Maybe when we get to the ground floor we'll find the last four levels all in one great big shit-scary package."

"That's the spirit," said Dev, setting off again with Richard limping behind. "Perhaps we could pass the time guessing what we're going to find."

"Monsters, zombies, fungi," Richard mused as he hobbled along, doing his best to ignore the creeping ache in his thigh, and trying ever harder to ignore the cause of it. "Maybe it'll be something even further down the evolutionary scale."

"Primitive plant life, you mean?" said Sandra.

"Yes, or possibly something even older?" Dev suggested. "Bacteria? Or viruses?"

As they reached the door to the second floor and eased it open a crack they realised they had all guessed wrong, as a hinged and chitinous limb the height of a man and bristling with hairs forced its way through.

"Close the door!" cried Sandra.

But it was too late. Dev was propelled backward and he cannoned into the wall behind him as something large and chittering knocked the door aside with one swipe of a powerful-looking claw. The insectoid creature squeezed the front part of its body through the doorway and regarded the prostrate pathologist with seven sets of multi-faceted compound eyes. For a split second all was still as the creature, its shining violet carapace flecked with orange, raised its claws to deal its victim a deathly blow.

The first to react was Sandra, taking out her knife and slashing at one of the creature's upper limbs. She struck it with such force that the pincer it was waving in the air came away at the joint and fell to the floor with a clatter. Foul-smelling liquid spurted from the amputated stump, splashing the wall to Dev's left. Almost immediately, the fungal growths they had seen upstairs began to take root and multiply on the whitewashed brickwork.

"Dev! Move your arse!"

Dev didn't need any further encouragement. As the creature raised its remaining claw, the pincers open in readiness to tear the flesh from his bones, Dev shoved himself to the left, propelling himself first into a crouching, and then quickly into a standing position.

The creature's many eyes were still on him, however, and so when Sandra struck at the junction between its head and thorax, burying her knife as deeply as she could before pulling it out again, all the monster could do was emit an ear-splitting screech as it thrashed about, copious quantities of fungal fluid spraying from its neck wound. Dev ducked out of the way as the thing gave a final spasm and then fell onto the concrete steps with a bone-jarring crunch.

Richard had managed to stagger to the stairway door and push it closed, although not before catching a glimpse of what lay beyond in the second floor corridor. The lights were still working in there, and their artificial glow made the vista on which he found himself looking seem even weirder. He saw creatures that resembled mud-coloured bats, but with too many legs, and jaws the shape of an alligator's; a horde of tiny crawling, clicking things were feasting on whatever had collapsed in a corner three feet away; squirming creatures that resembled mustard-coloured snakes, but which were far too long and thin and possessed heads that lacked eyes. Each time one of the blind writhing things collided with a clicking creature, a sucker opened up where the mouth should have been and consumed it.

That was all he saw before he slammed the door, but it was more than enough.

He was about to tell the others what he had seen but Sandra was already pointing in horror to the insectoid monstrosity she had killed.

The orange-purple carapace was dissolving.

No, not dissolving.

Fragmenting.

As they watched, the creature's exoskeleton broke up into tiny pieces, which then themselves fragmented, forming uniform hexagonal shapes no larger than the head of a match.

Then each one revealed the tiny legs it had been

concealing beneath its armour plating, and tested the air with tiny clubbed antennae.

Then they swarmed towards them.

"What the fuck are they?" Sandra was already backing away.

"They eat human flesh!" said Richard, circling the mass of tiny creatures that had, until a few seconds ago been much larger and just as deadly. He and Dev made it to the stairs together. "At least, the ones back down the corridor were."

The three of them ran back the way they had come, the swarm coming after them with frightening speed. In a moment they were back at the floor above, falling into the fungoid jungle.

Richard slammed the door behind them.

"What the hell are we going to do now?"

Dev eyed the moist environment ahead of them. Greenish fluid dripped from the fleshy stalactites.

"I don't fancy staying here," he said.

"We may not have a choice," said Sandra, using her fingers to rip a slab of the stuff from a nearby wall. It came away from the concrete like dead flesh from infected bone.
"Jesus Christ, Sandra!" Richard couldn't believe what she had just done. "That stuff could be poisonous!"

Sandra was too busy stuffing it under the crack in the door to reply straight away. "What else do you suggest we use to try and stop those things from getting in here?" she asked. "Your coat's out of action and Dev and I are down to the bare minimum."

Dev looked at his shirt sleeves and shrugged. "Richard's got a point though, Sandra."

"Well it's done now, isn't it?" Sandra coughed and wiped

her hands on her surgical scrub top. "They'll probably eat through it in a bit but hopefully it'll give us long enough to get away."

"I'll say it again." Dev was looking ahead of them once more. This time he pointed for emphasis. "I don't fancy staying here, but are you suggesting we try and carve our way through that?"

There was silence apart from the incessant dripping of fungal fluid, and a buzzing sound from the other side of the door.

"We might have to," said Richard, eventually. "In fact, for the first time this evening, I've got a bit of a plan."

"Just a bit of one?" Sandra sneezed. "How's that going to help?"

"Better than none at all.' Dev shot Sandra a frown. "What's are you thinking, Richard?"

"The book wants to get back to Arthur Lipscomb's room, right?"

"Right." Dev didn't sound at all sure about where this was headed.

"And we need to get to the ground floor to get his blood from the emergency room so we can do his summoning ritual, only backwards - right?"

"Right." Sandra sounded equally uninspired.

"All I am suggesting," said Richard, getting to his feet, "is that we split up. You two get downstairs. There must be another staircase up ahead somewhere, hopefully one that isn't crawling with purple shield bugs that want to eat you. I'll press on until I get back to the room Arthur disappeared from."

"Hang on a minute." Dev was scratching his head. "For a minute there I thought you were suggesting Sandra and I face almost certain death by getting to where all three of us are meant to be going, while you go and face definite certain death by going back to the room where you've already said something big and horrible tried to get you when you read that book."

"I've got an idea," said Richard. "I might be able to get that book to take me to wherever Arthur's gone."

"Which will help us how?" From Sandra's expression it was clear she also thought Richard had gone mad.

"If I can talk to him, get him to help us," Richard looked around him. "Maybe it'll give us an edge in trying to change all this back."

"It'll give you a knife edge," said Dev. "One that'll be used to cut your own throat."

"You must admit I'm slowing you down." Richard gave him a wistful grin. "And the further away we move from that side room the more pain the book is going to cause me. I can feel it. Better to embrace my fate and try and turn it to our advantage, don't you think?"

"No, I don't think." Was it Richard's imagination or was there the hint of a tear in the orthopaedic registrar's eyes? "Three is always going to be better than two against all this fucking nonsense."

"Richard's got a point, Sandra." Dev's voice was solemn. "He's going to slow us down more and more the further down we go. Admittedly it's a crazy idea, but no more than anything else I've witnessed here tonight."

"And if I succeed, " Richard gave them his most hopeful look, even though he was aware it probably looked vaguely absurd. "I'll see you in the car park outside and we can all go for a pint."

Sandra thumped him.

Richard couldn't help but smile as he flinched. "Is that because you'll be glad to see the back of me?"

"It's because if I don't see you again I'll be coming after you to hit you even harder," she said, giving him another whack for good measure.

"In that case I'll make sure I get back in double quick time," Richard replied.

He didn't expect her to hug him, nor did he expect it to last as long as it did.

"Don't you dare tell anyone I did that," said Sandra once it was over.

"Of course not," said Richard.

Sandra glared at Dev.

"Oh I promise," he said. "I don't want to risk getting thumped as well."

The three friends regarded the murky gloom ahead of them. Dev to the left, Richard to the right, and Sandra in the middle.

"Ready?" Richard asked.

"No," said Dev.

"Ready as I'll ever be," said Sandra.

"Then let's get going."

CHAPTER ELEVEN

They had to move slowly. Creeping growths had erupted on the walls and were making their way, slowly but inevitably, down and across the ground. Although Richard had assumed they were some kind of fungus, it was difficult not to think of them as cancers, malignant growths of both plaster and concrete that had burst forth from material that was normally inorganic, but which had acquired life as a consequence of whatever power it was that by now must have spread through the entire hospital.

"You know what I'm thinking?" Dev asked.

Richard nodded. "Cancer."

"What I'd give to be able to look at a piece of this stuff under the microscope." Dev whistled. "It would probably make my career if I ever live to have one."

Sandra pushed aside a cluster of red-brown tendrils that had erupted from a light fitting, the bulb broken but the electricity somehow still illuminating the filament, bathing the area an eerie shade of burnt umber that almost evoked warmth.

The tendrils retracted as she touched them, reacting to the pressure of her fingertips by secreting a sticky substance. Sandra wiped them with a tissue and then threw the crumpled paper to the ground.

"I said you shouldn't touch this stuff," Richard cautioned her. "We're bound to come across some that's poisonous."

"Probably sooner rather than later." Dev pointed as, on the floor nearby, a growth the colour of embalmed flesh extended blue-grey hyphae and snatched the tissue up. The three of them watched in horror as it dissolved and was absorbed.

"The tentacles upstairs absorbed blood and flesh," he said. "My guess is these things will soon evolve to that level."

"What are they?" Sandra deftly avoided another hanging gathering of ropey, anaemic-looking tendrils, these ones lined with tiny hooks.

"What Richard said, I think," Dev replied. "Extensions of the building itself. Cancers, mutations, aberrations. It's as if something had infected this building at a microscopic level and is trying to change its entire structure." He looked at Sandra. "It wouldn't surprise me at all if the people who died upstairs gave the thing enough energy to spread through the rest of the building."

"But why did it start there?" Richard was bringing up the rear, his limp far less pronounced now that he was nearing the place the book wanted him to go. "Why not on this floor where Arthur Lipscomb performed the ritual? Or the next floor up?"

Dev shrugged. "How should I know? And don't forget the girl I was supposed to be dissecting. She might have been the thing's first effort and when we defeated it whatever nebulous form of energy Mr Lipscomb managed to bring into this world searched for sustenance elsewhere."

"Well it certainly found it." Sandra coughed as a flurry of tiny spores erupted from something she had just trodden on. "You know, I'm beginning to wonder if coming this way was such a good idea."

"The next staircase should be along here, somewhere," said Richard, looking to his left. "I used to come this way. It's the quickest route to the blood gas analyser."

"That's right," Dev mused. "We're still close to the respiratory wards."

"So?"

Dev pointed to where Sandra had just stepped. "I don't think breathing in those spores, or even touching them, is going to be such a good idea. We've managed to avoid them so far but if we have to go much further we might be glad of oxygen tanks and masks."

"Hopefully that won't be necessary." Richard was pointing to the side. "I think we've found it."

Sandra peered at the fungus-smothered recess Richard was indicating. "All I can see is more of the same shit," she said.

"Behind all of that." Richard waved his right hand in the general direction while Dev and Sandra remained unimpressed. "You'll need to cut some of that stuff away. Have you got any gloves left, Dev?"

It so happened he did. One pair.

"So Sandra can use her knife to cut and you can pull it away."

Sandra looked at him incredulously. "And what are you going to do?'

Richard looked at the corridor ahead of him. The light was much dimmer, and there was a lot more of the fungus. "Something I really don't want to," he said. "And just in case it all goes horribly wrong you two need to get away from this floor as quickly as you can."

"I thought it would be more difficult to part ways." Sandra already had her knife out. "But if you think I'm going to follow you into that bloody jungle down there you've got another thing coming."

Richard smiled. "Don't worry. I'm going to wait here until I'm sure you're through. I need both of you to get that circle drawn."

There was a pause, and then Dev held out his hand.

Richard took it and gave it a hearty shake.

"No," said Dev. "What I meant was I need your phone with the pictures on. I'm not going to be able to draw that thing from memory."

Despite having tackled undead corpses, blood drinking tentacled things and insects from another dimension, the crushing embarrassment Richard suddenly felt was almost on a par and he could not help but emit a high-pitched giggle of hysterical laughter.

"Steady on, cowboy," said Dev as the phone was handed over. "Remember - you need to keep that sanity if you're going to have any chance of finding our Mr Lipscomb."

"Oh I don't know." Richard patted the book in his pocket. The pain it had been causing him had now dulled to an ache that he could almost describe as gentle. "Loss of sanity might be a definite advantage."

It took Dev and Sandra just under two minutes to clear away the growths from where Richard had thought the nearest stairwell lay. Once they had removed enough to expose the door and its hinges Dev gave it an experimental push and Sandra had a look through the crack that was created.

"Lights are on," she said.

"Great." Dev breathed a sigh of relief.

"And no insects, tentacles or fungus that I can see, either."

"You'd best get going," said Richard. "It's probably not going to stay that way for long."

They all knew they wanted a longer goodbye than they dared allow themselves, and so it was with a heavy heart that Richard gave his friends a single wave as they disappeared to make their way to the ground floor.

Then he turned to face the corridor ahead of him.

The encroaching darkness wasn't a problem, not after what he had endured upstairs. Whatever floor space remained had given in to a covering of wet, grey fungal growths and the increasingly spongy feeling beneath his feet didn't bother him too much either.

What bothered him was the smell.

He hadn't noticed it so much when Dev and Sandra had been there, but now they were gone it had suddenly overwhelmed him. A rank, dusty, pungent odour redolent of vegetables left to rot in a sack, or fruit sealed in a Tupperware container and forgotten about until weeks later. The odour caught him in the back of the throat, and he tried to blot out images of tiny hyphae trying to attach themselves to the mucosa of his larynx, anchoring themselves in his throat and taking root, growing the same foul thing inside him as he was stepping on right now.

He coughed again, inspecting the air created by his expelled breath for any traces of the spores he was determined not to allow inside himself.

This might not be as easy as he had thought.

Richard took another step forward. The atmosphere was almost stifling, the stink of mould and rot so intense he could almost reach out and push a finger through it. From memory he knew that the orthopaedic wing was on the other side of the hospital from respiratory medicine. The former temporary residence of Mr Arthur Lipscomb was going to take some getting to.

Richard removed his white coat. The book was happy to let him now that he was going in what it obviously considered the right direction. He took the volume from the coat and put it in his trouser pocket, where it nestled unobtrusively, causing him neither an ounce of pain nor any disability.

Then he wrapped the coat around his right wrist and used the improvised club to push aside the heavier of the hanging tendrils. The tips leaked more of the brown fluid onto the material, staining it the colour of dead leaves and releasing an odour that was even more intense.

As he made his way through the primitive jungle that had once been Floor 3 of Northcote Hospital, Richard could not help but marvel at how much it had changed. Where there had once been doorways to wards he now saw recesses clogged with fungus and clotted with hyphae. In the few instances where the cancerous growths had not totally obliterated the entrances, Richard was able to catch a glimpse of the wards themselves, where the floors and walls had fallen victim to the same malignant process.

And as for their human occupants...

Richard knew he needed to get to Lipscomb's room as quickly as possible, but he simply couldn't pass by one of the open wards and not check it for any sign of survivors.

Once he had, he wished he had ignored the impulse to do so.

The way into the ward was much like the corridor, the walls layered with fungus, noxious fluid dripping from the ceiling and feeding the unsavoury growths that were creeping across the floor.

It was the nurses' desk, and the patient bays that made Richard feel sick.

The eruption of the tumours that now encased much of what surrounded him must have happened very quickly indeed, because neither the patients, who were still in their beds, nor the two nurses on night shift who were trapped at their posts, could have had much time to react. The insidious malignancy had moved fast, trapping each patient and plastering them to the mattress while probing hyphae had entered their mouths and noses, the results of their activities bearing fruit in the stalk-like bodies which had erupted from their victims' eyes.

One of the nurses must have tried to phone for help, but

it looked as if something had burst from the receiver and entered her ear, spreading over the right side of her skull and reducing it to a dry powder that crumbled as Richard watched. The other nurse was so deeply buried beneath layers of pallid fleshy excrescences that it was difficult to believe there was a human being under there.

As he retreated, Richard put the muffled sobs he thought he could hear down to his imagination.

He would not be investigating any of the other wards.

Further on down the main corridor the growths cleared a little, and the light became brighter, enough that Richard wondered if perhaps his journey might not be the hell he had been expecting. Then he turned the corner.

Up ahead, about a hundred feet away, he could see his destination. The way into Yew Tree ward looked surprisingly free from the cancerous rot that had infected the passageway from which he had just come. He had to get there first, though, and that might prove difficult.

Between the floor on which he was standing, and the white tiles outside Yew Tree ward, stretched a pool of blackness.

The lights were on, the walls and ceiling were white and, apart from an occasional fleshy eruption here and there, unsullied. The floor, however, had been replaced by a one hundred foot stretch of what looked like black ink.

It probably wasn't though, Richard thought as he unwound the white coat from his arm and laid it on the ground in front of him, just to see what might happen.

The black liquid flooded over it and a chemical smell of burning cotton assailed his nostrils.

Richard looked over his shoulder to see that the way he had come was now blocked by a thick nodular mass of impenetrable, fungating tumour tissue.

John Llewellyn Probert

No choice for it but to keep going, then.

He judged the distance ahead. If he ran as fast as he could, and took long strides, he might just be able to clear it before the soles of his shoes (and those of his feet) were dissolved by the black oily acid. There was nothing else he could do. He took a step back, taking care not to come into contact with the glistening wall of bulging growths, and hurled himself forward.

It was like trying to run on wet tar.

As soon as his right foot touched the substance, he could feel it being sucked down, and the leather of his shoe dissolving beneath him. But there was no turning back, and so he carried on, left foot, right foot, each step an effort so great he wondered if he might die of exhaustion before the acid got to him.

He was halfway down the corridor when the things began to emerge.

'Emerge' wasn't quite the right word for the coiling, slithering extensions of the sticky black surface. It was more like they had arisen from the tar itself, were part of the creature that Richard was treading on. He had a sudden, horrifying realisation that the thing he was dragging himself across was the tongue of some monstrous creature, its surface like flypaper, and that the coiling, snake-like protuberances now appearing either side of him were accessory organs designed to keep the prey in the organism's mouth while it slowly digested it.

But he couldn't give up. He dodged the black, coiling rope-like appendages, pulling his feet across the sticky, tarry surface as quickly as he could. He looked up and saw Yew Tree ward ahead of him.

Not far to go now.

But what might be lying in wait for him when he arrived? Richard decided it was best not to think about that as, with a final, immense effort, he threw himself clear of the limit of the tongue-thing and onto the pristine white floor tiles.

He lay there, panting and marvelling that there appeared to be no immediate danger here. It was only after a while that he felt something strange against his right thigh. A peculiar quivering from what lay in his pocket.

Still lying on what seemed like the relative safety of the floor outside Yew Tree ward, Richard put his hand into his pocket, and drew out the book.

The fleshy cover, its tendon-like bindings, and pages the texture of old dry skin, were moving. The whole volume was gently pulsating as if it had a life of its own.

For a moment he imagined it was laughing at him.

Right, he thought, stuffing it back into his pocket and getting to his feet. *That's quite enough from you. Time to see if Mr Lipscomb is at home to visitors.*

The doors to Yew Tree ward appeared to be relatively unscathed, apart from a couple of deep jagged scratch marks in the wood. Richard hoped that whatever had made them wasn't waiting for him within as he pushed the doors open.

And entered a world no living person had ever seen before.

CHAPTER TWELVE

Dev and Sandra made it down to the second floor without incident. Neither of them spoke as they pointedly ignored the door that would likely take them into a world of giant insectoid creatures and tiny, voraciously hungry parasites. They were too preoccupied with thoughts of the friend they had left behind, even though they knew there was nothing they could have done to persuade him to go with them.

"I wonder what's on the next floor down?" Those were the first words Sandra had spoken since they had left Richard behind.

"Let's just hope that whatever it is, it hasn't managed to get into this stairwell," said Dev. "Let's get past the first floor door as quickly as possible and save our energies for whatever we're going to have to face on the ground."

A malignant green ichor was seeping beneath the stairwell door to the first floor. Tiny granules moved within it, glittering in the artificial light. Despite what he had said, Dev couldn't help but slow down to inspect it.

"Come on!" Sandra was pulling at his arm.

"Those tiny sparkling dots," Dev said with amazement. "They're creatures. Tiny organisms living in that...that stuff."

"And they can probably grow and turn into any one of the god-awful things we've seen upstairs, so let's keep going, shall we?"

Another glop of the thick slimy fluid bubbled under the door and Dev didn't need to be told twice.

It wasn't long before they reached the ground floor. The

stairwell came to an end and they found themselves faced with the door that led out of it.

"It looks okay." Sandra was reaching out to turn the handle.

"Doesn't mean it is, though," Dev warned her. "Be careful."

The first thing to hit them when the door opened was the smell.

"It's like a bloody garden centre." Sandra wrinkled her nose.

"More like a prehistoric jungle." Dev sniffed and then sneezed."Remind me not to accept any garden party invitations from you."

"What makes you think I'd invite you?" she replied, her face grim.

Much of the structure of the ground floor had vanished, to be replaced by bubbling pools of foul-smelling brown liquid. Here and there heaps of tan-coloured mud rose no higher than waist height and gave off a moist vapour that added to the miasma. They looked down to find that they were walking on earth, strewn with small rocks and the bones of tiny animals.

"Where are we?" Sandra turned round to look behind them. The doorway by which they had entered was now obscured by the mixture of vapours and gases prevalent in the atmosphere.

"Somewhere very old, or possibly very young," said Dev. "Almost as if this whole place is trying to evolve from the ground up but keeps getting it wrong."

"What?"

Dev shook his head. "Just thinking aloud, sorry. Do you have any idea where the emergency department is down here?"

Sandra was too busy looking up.

"I don't remember the ceiling ever being this high," she said.

Dev shrugged. He didn't remember the light coming from what looked like distant suns in a milky sky, either, but they couldn't worry about that right now.

"Do you really think the emergency department is still here?" Sandra sounded convinced that it wasn't.

"We have to count on it," said Dev. "Don't lose hope. Some parts of this building have been altered and others have been left relatively unchanged. Let's hope where we need to go has been left untouched for the moment. Now where do we need to go?"

Sandra looked behind her again. The miasma had cleared a little and the door was visible once again. "If that's the exit staircase that brought us down from respiratory then where we're standing would once have been out-patients." She closed her eyes for a moment. "That means the emergency department should be straight ahead and to the left."

"How many paces, roughly?"

Sandra blinked. "How the fuck should I know? I never count the steps I take to get there. I'm usually too busy running."

Dev was insistent. "But if we keep going in a straight line from here—"

"—if we keep that door in sight, yes—"

"—if we keep that door in sight and keep straight, and then at some point to be best guessed at by you we turn left, we should get there?"

"Yes," Sandra nodded. "If it is still there, of course."

Dev sighed. "Well, seeing as we really don't have

anything better to do, let's try and find it, shall we?"

They continued walking in a straight line away from the staircase door. Soon they were far enough away from it for it to have disappeared into the distance. From then on it was guesswork.

After another ten minutes they came to a halt.

"Shouldn't we be turning left soon?" Dev asked, coughing. The heavy vapours were starting to irritate his lungs.

"We probably should have a while back." Sandra didn't sound too hopeful. "To be honest, Dev, I'm lost. I don't know where we should turn and I don't know how I'm supposed to be able to tell. All I can say is that we'll have to very soon."

"Why?"

Sandra pointed ahead of them to the wall of drab brown concrete that blocked their path. It extended both left and right as far as they could see. The wall must have been at least thirty feet high.

Something was moving behind it.

Something vast and thunderous.

Something that was heaving itself against the barrier and causing chips of rock and dust to tumble to the muddy ground below.

"Must be one of the hospital's supporting walls," said Dev. "For some reason it hasn't been obliterated like everything else."

There was another ear-splitting thump as whatever was trying to make its way through cannoned against it again.

And again.

A vertical crack appeared close to where they were

standing.

Sandra took Dev's hand. "Let's get moving."

Dev was happy to be led as Sandra dragged him onwards, talking as they broke into a jog.

"If that's one of the main supporting walls," she said, "then the emergency department should be down here and on the left. We overshot it but it doesn't surprise me."

"How the hell are we going to know when we're there?"

They knew.

Dev nearly tripped over a patient trolley, half buried in the primordial mud, its exposed part already rusting in the unnatural atmosphere. Around them lay other pieces of equipment; a defibrillator machine covered in pale brown dust, an operating table bent in half as if by huge, supernaturally powerful hands.

"We must have come past the Radiology department on the way here," Dev breathed, remembering the clumsy rock formations they had passed that must actually have been fossilised equipment for taking X-Rays. "Everything's still here."

"For the moment," Sandra was already searching through the detritus of half-buried cabinets and boxes as the incessant hammering and cracking noises behind them continued. "Help me look through these."

It was difficult to know where to start. The nearest cabinet was the size of a small wardrobe and buried up to the handles. Dev aimed a hefty kick at the left hand door but only succeeded in hurting himself.

"Not that one. It's full of dressings." Sandra pointed "Try that one over there."

A locker of similar size but far more accessible loomed ahead, only slightly buried but angled such that the slightest pressure could bring the whole lot toppling onto him. Dev reached out tentatively and pulled the handle. It came open with a protest but he was eventually able to create enough of a gap that he could see inside.

The shelves within had collapsed, and now a jumble of white metal grids and what they had been holding lay at the bottom. Dev pulled the doors apart a little and peered more closely.

Bags.

He peered more closely still, aware that the crushing pressure from the forced open doors could probably break his neck if his strength failed.

Blood bags.

The ground heaved.

"Sandra!" he yelled and tried to hold the doors apart while the surface he was standing on began to buck and undulate. "Sandra I think I've found some blood!"

Sandra staggered across the shifting landscape towards him, falling to one side and then the other as she strove to maintain her balance. Dev maintained his position as she rooted around in the depths of what had until recently been the emergency department's blood store.

"Hurry up!" Dev was biting his lip as he lurched from side to side and the cabinet with him. He wouldn't be able to hold on much longer and if he let go with Sandra still in there—

Sandra was out, holding aloft three red bags with a heavy 'A' symbol stamped on them.

"These should do!" Sandra had to shout to be heard above the noise coming from the shifting ground around her. She held up three glass tubes that contained something that looked very similar. Written on the side, in Richard's tiny but legible capitals were the words 'Arthur Lipscomb'. "I found them over there!"

The ground shifted again and Sandra fell backwards, taking care to hold her precious cargo away from her. "What the hell is going on now?"

"I think this place is shifting again, to try and make it more like what it wants and less like what we're used to seeing." Dev watched as the ground beneath the half-buried trolley split and consumed it. "It needs to get rid of all evidence that we were ever here."

Sandra pushed herself to her feet. "In that case we'd better get on with this," she said, tearing at the seal on the first blood bag. "It doesn't look as if we have much time."

Dev resisted the urge to say it looked as if they didn't have any time at all. Instead he held the bag open for Sandra while she unstoppered the specimen tubes belonging to Arthur Lipscomb and poured in the contents. Then, making sure he had the top held tightly closed, he shook the bag up.

"Let's hope Richard's having some luck upstairs," he said.

But at that moment, Richard was dealing with problems of his own.

CHAPTER THIRTEEN

As soon as he had entered Yew Tree ward, Richard knew everything had been changed by the power Arthur Lipscomb had called into being. Little of what he could recognise as being part of a normal hospital remained. Instead, he found himself walking though a green-tinted otherworld, in which the expanded and distorted landscape was furnished with queer abstractions and deformed impressions of what had been there before. As his eyes adjusted to the dimness, he began to see bays of beds designed for abnormally tall, thin creatures, arranged in rows that stretched to the horizon. The mattresses seemed to be made of the same malignant fungal material he had encountered outside. The bodies they were intended for lay not on but above them, suspended in mid-air, their forms only a semblance of human beings, twisted and stretched, corkscrewed and remoulded into things horrible to gaze upon.

As Richard made his way between them he almost tripped over a slumped shape that was dragging itself across the ground, its sightless eyes determining its direction by the myriad thread-like feelers that had erupted from its eyelids. It was only when it looked up that he realised the thing had once been Kerry Morris, the Health Care Auxiliary who had helped him with Mr Lipscomb earlier on.

His revulsion dissipated by the realisation of who it was, Richard did his best not to cause her any harm as he stepped over her, noting with infinite sadness her sealed-over ears, the strange wormlike organs that clustered at the back of her neck, and her limbs, now little more than useless jointed flippers that appeared to possess neither bone nor cartilage.

Arthur Lipscomb's side room had been to the right and round a corner. Richard did his best to ignore what the main ward had become. and turned in that direction.

He found his way blocked by a forest of criss-crossing spikes.

They rose out of the floor and stretched far up into the vastly high ceiling over his head. As he examined one he realised they weren't made of metal, but more something resembling split bamboo. Then he realised.

They were fingernails.

Infinitely long, unnaturally thick fingernails.

Richard reached out, grasped one firmly, and broke it.

A scream echoed somewhere above him, sending crawling chills through his gut and giving his spine the wet, cold feeling of something long drowned.

Unperturbed, he guessed that he must be going in the right direction. Richard reached out again, grasped another, and broke that too.

This time the scream was more drawn out, more pleading, more human.

Trying to trick me, thought Richard, *or stop me. Well, the time for games is over.*

This time he grabbed several in each fist, took a deep breath, and then snapped them as savagely as he could.

The noise was deafening.

Richard put his hands over his ear as he pushed his way through the splintered remains of what had been blocking his path, the light dimming further as he did so.

Eventually, everything ahead went completely black.

Deprived of his sight, Richard turned around.

The distorted place from which he had come had vanished.

He felt a twinge of panic as he realised he was trapped in silent darkness, every sense lost to him except the feeling that he was walking on floor tiles.

And kicking aside small pieces of gravel, dust, and rubble.

And what felt like scraps of rags.

There was a light up ahead. Far away at first but rapidly increasing in size until it was as big as a silver coin, high in the heavens above him.

It was the moon. A normal, natural, perfectly full moon.

Shining down through a grime-streaked window into a high up floor of what had to be a condemned block of flats.

Richard grimaced at the rubbish on the floor, a mixture of drug-takers' leavings, squatters' fires and broken pieces of the building that could no longer muster the strength to be a part of it.

But still, here he was in a normal building, looking out of a normal filthy window at some brilliantly normal stars and a normal moon.

"You're not really here, you know."

Richard turned. The old man had crept up on him without making a sound.

"By which I mean you're not really on the fifth floor of Appleton Court on Northcote Park estate. It looks very much like it. Like I remember it, anyway, but it isn't."

Richard didn't know what to say. "Mr Lipscomb, I—"

"You don't have to say anything." Lipscomb gave a dismissive wave. Richard couldn't help notice that the nails of each finger were absent and the tips were crusted with

135

dried blood. "This?" His observation had been spotted. "You did this. Trying to get in here, trying to get to me. I screamed and screamed but you still came."

"I'm sorry. I'm so sorry."

Mr Lipscomb didn't seem too bothered. "Don't think anything of it," he said. "I've suffered far worse since I was imprisoned here."

"Imprisoned?"

The old man nodded. "I was promised so much, and rewarded with so little. But that's so often the way of the world, isn't it? Why should we be surprised if other worlds, other universes, work in the same way?"

Realisation dawned. "You're trapped here?"

Lipscomb gave him a maniacal grin. "Both my reward, and my punishment. My reward because I don't get to become subject to the way your world is changing now - and it is changing, my boy, and don't think there's anything you can do to stop it - and my punishment because I did not complete the ritual in the way They wished." He spread his bloodstained fingers. "I did my best, and I was offered so much if I did my part correctly."

Richard took the book from his pocket. "This is what offered you things, isn't it?"

Both the old man and the book seemed to recoil from each other at once. Richard hung on to the spongy, foul-smelling volume despite its beginning to secrete a sweaty grease that made it more difficult.

Lipscomb's eyes lit up. "Where did you get that?"

"From your hospital room. You left it behind in case you don't remember."

"It should have been consumed! As part of the ritual! Absorbed into the room like I was!" His eyes glittered as he stretched out a grimy hand. "Give it to me."

Richard stuffed it back into his pocket and tried to ignore the slimy cold feeling against his leg. "I think you've had that book for quite long enough."

Lipscomb shook his head. "You don't understand. If you have the book that means everything will be unstable, malformed. The other universe will be straining to right itself in our world. They cannot meet. One has to replace the other, not meld with it." He reached out with both hands but Richard was too quick and avoided his flailing grasp. "It has to be stopped or both universes will be destroyed."

"Well at least we agree it has to be stopped." Richard continued to back away as the old man continued to stalk him. "Do you know how to?"

"No." Lipscomb's expression was too revealingly cunning. "But if you let me see the book I can find out for you."

Richard shook his head. "Why don't you tell me which page to look on and I can do it myself?"

"You fucking idiot!" The words came out as a hiss. "Do you really think you can learn to do in minutes what it took me years to achieve? Give me that book now and pray for a swift and simple death, not like the ones your friends will suffer, if they haven't already."

"If you get your hands on it do you really think the book is going to treat you any better than it already has?" Richard was up against the window now, and the light rendered Lipscomb an unearthly shade of silver as the old man grasped at him.

"Better than it will treat you, boy," came the snarled reply as Lipscomb prepared to hurl himself forwards.

There was nothing else Richard could do. With the book straining to get out of his pocket, he raised his arm to defend himself, intending to push his attacker away as gently as possible. The old man was even frailer than he looked and fell to the ground with an unhealthy crunch.

"I'm sorry." Richard could not help but feel guilty over what he'd done, and he reached out to help Lipscomb up.

As he leaned over, the book fell from his pocket. Richard flicked it away with his foot, but not far enough. The old man's eyes glittered as he tried to crawl towards it. The fall had broken his right leg and it hung uselessly as he dragged the rest of his body toward the volume. It was bathed in moonlight, and the silver glow made the book look bigger.

No, Richard realised with horror, the book was bigger.

And growing all the time.

"Mine," was all poor old Arthur Lipscomb could croak as he reached for it with his crusted fingertips; as the book, now the size of a coffin, flipped open its cover and pages came crawling forth, like limping, dying seagulls, to envelop him.

The old man turned to look at Richard. "You're a part of this now," he said. "You always were."

He screamed once as the pages dragged him back into the book's interior.

Then the cover slammed shut.

And the room changed.

The rubbish, the fallen masonry, the crumbling plaster, the shredded furniture, had all gone.

So had the walls and the ceiling.

Richard looked down. The floor on which he was standing was now made of rough, uneven blue rock. The stars in the night sky above him had changed and the moon was just a sliver of its former glory.

He approached one of the edges of the square of stone

on which he now found himself, only to encounter a sheer drop on each side. Far below, the landscape looked untouched by modern man.

A gentle breeze blew as Richard tried to come to terms with his current situation. The tower block had gone and so had the book, taking with it poor old Arthur Lipscomb, presumably to the dimension from which it had come.

Leaving Richard standing atop a one hundred foot high menhir.

The wind was picking up. Richard made a careful inspection of every side, crawling gingerly to the edge and looking over, before concluding that there was no way down.

He got to his feet. What was he to do? Had he saved the hospital? Or had his efforts been in vain? Were Dev and Sandra currently battling creatures from another dimension while trying to draw the circle using Mr Lipscomb's blood? How would he ever know?

Only one thing was certain, he was going to get nowhere hanging around here.

With courage borne of all the things that had happened to him tonight, Richard took careful steps to one edge of the blue menhir.

Then he took a deep breath.

And jumped.

CHAPTER FOURTEEN

As soon as Dev had begun pouring the blood, the ground on which both he and Sandra were standing had started to convulse. It was all they could do to stand upright as they were shaken by wave upon wave of jarring tremors emanating from far beneath them. Cracks were appearing in the scorched earth, revealing squirming things with clicking mandibles and segmented bodies, clambering over one another with their myriad legs in their hurry to get to their victims on the surface.

"Stop staring and get on with it!"

Dev tore his eyes away from the crawling subterranean creatures and completed the circle. Then he looked once more at the picture on Richard's mobile, held out for him by Sandra, who had her eyes fixed on him.

"Two lines like this." Dev shouted as he drew, more to maintain his concentration than to confirm with Sandra that he was doing the right thing. "Then one at an angle. A curlicue thing with the tail missed off, and a triangle with a weird shape inside it."

They carried on, Sandra occasionally checking the image to make sure Dev was copying it correctly.

The cracks in the ground were growing larger and the writhing bodies were now much closer to the surface.

In the distance there was a terrible crash as the wall came down, freeing whatever enormity it had been holding back. The sound of tremendous hoofbeats shook the ground and caused the cracks to spread all the more rapidly.

Finally, Dev was finished.

"What do we do now?" Sandra yelled.

Dev looked around him. "There are probably some words we have to say."

"Like what?"

"I don't know! Can you read anything off the phone?"

Sandra squinted while trying to maintain her balance. "I can't make out anything on here." She tapped the screen and it changed to the same image from a different angle. Then a third, which was a closeup of the circle.

Tiny lettering could be seen etched around its circumference.

"Oh well done, Richard," she breathed as she held the phone up to show Dev. "There's something on here."

Dev looked behind him. The hoofbeats were getting louder, and the horizon began to darken. From above came a blast of hot, ungodly wind.

"Hurry up!" he shouted as the wind became stronger, turning into a gust from the heavens that, combined with the quaking ground, caused them both to fall to their knees.

From way above them a tiny dot appeared, rapidly increasing in size.

"Where should I start?" Sandra was turning the phone this way and that.

The horizon got darker.

The hoofbeats grew louder.

The dot increased in size.

"Anywhere!" Dev tried to get to his feet but another tremor forced him back to the ground. "Anywhere and just keep going, over and over, round and round! But make sure you read it backwards!"

Sandra started. She was only a few words in when Dev

141

realised that the dot that was rapidly descending towards them had arms and legs.

Before Dev had time to realise who it was, Richard landed on the circle with a thump, kicking up dust, smearing the blood pattern. He was still alive, and as he tried to move a crack opened in the ground beneath him. Whatever lay within it bathed him in an angry red glow.

"Oh, fuck." Dev stared open-mouthed at the body of his friend.

"Keep reading!" Richard pointed to Sandra with a broken right arm, his other, useless, limbs trapped and crumpled beneath him.

Sandra hadn't stopped. Driven by some other power, she seemed helpless to

stop herself from chanting the gargling, glottal, almost unpronounceable words. Over and over, round and round.

And backwards.

As she read, the ground began to shudder and split. Then, with little warning, it came away and his body was supported by the rope-like threads of blood that now made up the circle.

"Give me you hand!" Dev's was outstretched to take hold of him but Richard shook his head.

"Not going to happen," he wheezed. "I'm what it needs."

Sandra was being drawn to the circle. She dropped the phone, no longer needing it. She had become an automaton, nothing more than a vehicle by which the words she was speaking could propagate themselves. With slow, deliberate steps she walked towards Richard. When she was close enough, whip-like cords of blood lashed out and enveloped her.

"Fucking hell, Sandra, no!"

But Dev's words went unheard.

Richard held her close and gave his friend one last final wink goodbye as the latticework of plasma enveloped them both and they plunged into the abyss below.

The crack in the ground through which they had fallen immediately sealed itself, leaving Dev standing alone on the quaking plain.

No, not alone.

Something was behind him.

Dev turned and, for a moment, a split second that would remain with him throughout this life and into the next, he was witness to a vision of something immeasurable huge, something with horns and pounding limbs, and far too many of both, bearing down upon him.

Then he knew nothing more.

*

Dev woke to the stink of smoke. He assumed the piercing cries he could hear were those of yet more other-dimensional creatures until he looked up from the tarmac on which he was lying and saw the welter of red fire engines clustered around the hospital entrance.

"Best get you out of here, sir."

Dev had no strength to protest as two firemen lifted him to a safe distance at the far end of the car park. One stayed with him while the other went to help unload more hosepipes.

"Do you have any idea how it started?"

Dev shook his head. Not because he didn't know, but because no-one would ever believe him.

"The whole building's going up. You're lucky you weren't in there."

I was, Dev thought. *In ways you couldn't possibly imagine.*

That wasn't what he said, though. He licked his blistered lips and forced a drop of saliva down his throat to wet it sufficiently to form words. Even then it was still an effort to get them out.

"Let it burn."

The fireman either didn't hear him or pretended not to. He looked Dev in the eyes. "Are you going to be all right?"

Dev coughed and nodded. He was still too stunned to say anything else.

A thunder crack louder than any explosion rocked the ground.

"Jesus Christ." The fireman turned to look over his shoulder.

The six-storey tower block that was Northcote Hospital was moving.

The building shook. From its foundations to its roof the building juddered from side to side, almost as if something beneath the ground was trying to push it aside.

Cracks spread up from the A&E department and snaked through the concrete. Chunks of masonry fell to the ground as the cracks met and merged, forming a network of insidious destruction resembling a malignant spider's web.

Then the building began to come apart.

And something began to emerge from its depths.

Two huge, mottled hands as large as the building itself erupted from the structure in a shower of dust and rubble. The tapering claws searched blindly for a moment, seeking the two broken halves of the building. When they found what they were looking for, the roof of each half was grasped firmly, and what remained of the bricks and mortar of Northcote Hospital was pulled down into the smoking hole that had opened up beneath it.

The ground rumbled in the wake of this intrusion and then, just as it had with Richard and Sandra, it closed itself over, leaving not a trace that the building had ever existed.

"What the fuck happened there?" The fireman wasn't asking Dev, but the question deserved an answer anyway.

"Something that went wrong was taken care of," he said. "Our bodies do it all the time. It looks like the same thing can happen on a much larger scale, too."

"I don't know what you're on about, mate." The man was still in shock. "That whole fucking building just disappeared."

Dev shrugged. "I've seen worse," he said.

The fireman laid a hand on his shoulder. "You're obviously more shocked than I thought," he said. "You wait here and I'll get an ambulance to take you to...somewhere."

Dev watched him wander away to join the disorientated and mystified throng around the hospital site. After a while he got to his feet, grateful to be standing on good old-fashioned solid ground. He thought of Richard and Sandra, and of everyone else who had been in Northcote Hospital on what newspapers would no doubt soon be calling 'That Fateful Day'. He knew tears would come, but not just yet.

He turned and made his way to the hospital gates, past the reporters and television press vans that were already congregating there. The policemen keeping them out were too confused themselves to prevent him from leaving.

Dev thought about looking for his car, but decided against it. The sun was rising and it promised to be a beautiful day. He lived on the other side of the city and he had decided he was going to walk home.

It would take him ages, and he was going to need every

single step to help him recover.

Of course he had completely forgotten about Richard's phone, about the ritual images from the book. The ones that were still stored in its memory.

The images from the book had not forgotten about him, however.

They would let him get home, and give him some time to recover.

Then they would let him know that they were there.

And that they wished to try again.

ACKNOWLEDGEMENTS

Did you enjoy that? I sincerely hope you did. It was certainly a lot of fun to write, and the experience was made even more enjoyable this time around by a great team of people who all helped to bring this book into existence. So while I struggle into my dinner suit to give my thank you speech (actually I'm already wearing it as I type this but you guessed that, didn't you?) here, without any further ado, is a list of the everyone who deserves a big thank you for helping to bring Dead Shift into being:

My publisher Graeme Reynolds and his editorial team at Horrific Tales Publishing. Their attention to detail has helped to make this book better than I ever could have alone. Thanks Graeme - it's been a pleasure to work with you & the gang and I couldn't have wished for a better publishing experience.

My cover artist, Ben Baldwin, who supplied several different options for what would wrap around the pages I had written. They were all marvellous, but the one that graces the outside of this book is especially so, I think, so thank you Ben. If it really was true that you could judge a book by its cover then everyone would think this one was so excellent I could have got away without writing any insides for it.

My wife Kate aka Thana Niveau, who remains my first reader, my constant companion in the world of the weird, and the one who gets to hear what I've just written, even when she's in the middle of doing something else.

My friend Johnny Mains, without whom I would never have been written this book in the first place. Exactly why is a story sufficiently long that it would merit its own novella, but that can wait for another day.

John Llewellyn Probert

The surgical staff of Brunel Hospital Bristol, South Bristol Community Hospital, and Weston General Hospital, Weston super-Mare for indulging me every time I go off on one about what might happen if tentacles broke through the wall of the operating theatre I'm working in and other similar outbursts they probably don't have to put up with from anybody else. You're all wonderful and one of the best reasons for me to come to work.

And finally, if you're still with me, I need to thank you the reader. I've gone on a bit in other books about how the most important thing for me is that you put this or any other book of mine down feeling you've been entertained. I very much hope that's the case because you are the reason I do it. Take care of yourselves, be lovely to one another, and hopefully there will be another book along in a bit.

John Llewellyn Probert

Keeping a lookout over the Bristol Channel for trans-dimensional monsters

Somewhere in the South West of England

March 2016

THANK YOU FOR READING

Thank you for taking the time to read this book. We sincerely hope that you enjoyed the story and appreciate your letting us try to entertain you. We realise that your time is valuable, and without the continuing support of people such as yourself, we would not be able to do what we do.

As a thank you, we would like to offer you a free ebook from our range, in return for you signing up to our mailing list. We will never share your details with anyone and will only contact you to let you know about new releases.

You can sign up on our website

Http://www.horrifictales.co.uk

If you enjoyed this book, then please consider leaving a short review on Amazon, Goodreads or anywhere else that you, as a reader, visit to learn about new books. One of the most important parts about how well a book sells is how many positive reviews it has, so if you can spare a little more of your valuable time to share the experience with others, even if its just a line or two, then we would really appreciate it.

Thanks, and see you next time!

THE HORRIFIC TALES PUBLISHING TEAM

ABOUT THE AUTHOR

John Llewellyn Probert won the 2013 British Fantasy Award for his novella *The Nine Deaths of Dr Valentine* and 2015 saw the publication of its sequel, *The Hammer of Dr Valentine*. He is the author of over a hundred published short stories, six novellas and a novel, *The House That Death Built* (Atomic Fez). His first short story collection, *The Faculty of Terror*, won the 2006 Children of the Night award for best work of Gothic Fiction.

His latest stories can be found in *Best British Horror Volumes 1 & 2* (Salt Publishing), *Psychomania* and *Zombie Apocalypse! Endgame* (both Constable Robinson). Endeavour Press has published *Ward 19, Bloody Angels* and *The Pact* - three crime books featuring his pathologist heroine Parva Corcoran.

He is currently trying to review every cult movie in existence at his House of Mortal Cinema (**www.johnlprobert.blogspot.co.uk**) and everything he is up to writing-wise can be found at **www.johnlprobert.com**.

Future projects include a new short story collection, a lot more non-fiction writing, and a couple of novels.

He never sleeps.

ALSO FROM HORRIFIC TALES PUBLISHING

High Moor by Graeme Reynolds

High Moor 2: Moonstruck by Graeme Reynolds

High Moor 3: Blood Moon by Graeme Reynolds

Of A Feather by Ken Goldman

Whisper by Michael Bray

Echoes by Michael Bray

Voices by Michael Bray

Angel Manor by Chantal Noordeloos

Bottled Abyss by Benjamin Kane Ethridge

Lucky's Girl by William Holloway

The Immortal Body by William Holloway

Wasteland Gods by Jonathan Woodrow

COMING SOON

Song of the Death God by William Holloway

The Grieving Stones by Gary McMahon

Deadside Revolution by Terry Grimwood

The Rot by Paul Kane

http://www.horrifictales.co.uk